UNDER ARCHARD'S DOME

UNDER ARCHARD'S SPELL SERIES

COURTNEE TURNER HOYLE

PALE WOODS PUBLISHING

Under Archard's Dome

Under Archard's Spell, Book One

Copyright © June 16, 2023

Erwin, Tennessee by Courtnee Turner Hoyle

E-Book IBSN 979-8-9876468-4-7

Print IBSN 979-8-9876468-5-4

Cover design: Taylor Dawn, Sweet 15 Designs, LLC

Author Photo Credit: Tosha Cannon

— · —

To Tosha, who loves fantasy stories as much as me.
To Stereling, who watched dragons, werewolves, and unicorns with me
To Journee, who loved all the characters
To Jubilee, whose innocence is almost contagious
To all the people who suffer under the oppression of others. May you all be free.
To the readers who need to use this book as an escape.
May your mind be at peace.

— • —

UNDER ARCHARD'S DOME'S PLAYLIST

1. "We Are Who We Are" Missio

2. "Hotel California" The Eagles

3. "Softly" Arlo Parks

4. "Kids" MGMT

5. "Scary Monsters and Nice Sprites" Skrillex

6. "Uprising" Muse

7. "Midnight Hands" Rise Against

8. "Heat Waves" Glass Animals

9. "Love is a Battlefield" Pat Benatar

10. "Voices Carry" Til Tuesday

11. "Stargirl Interlude" The Weeknd (featuring Lana Del Ray)

12. "Kill EVERYBODY" Skrillex (Rymon's song)

13. "SNAP" Rosa Linn

14. "Hungry Like the Wolf" Duran Duran

15. "Love You to Death" Type O Negative

—•—

PROLOGUE

The members of the council looked down at me with varying expressions of sympathy, bewilderment, and contempt. I focused on
their stares with my fiery eyes, but I gave nothing away. I could feel
Rymon and Allistar behind me, but I wished they were in the Grand
Galley with the other graduates. As my closest friends, the council
had summoned them to the proceedings as witnesses.

Eight tribal counselors sat above me on a rounded dais, a wormy
chestnut podium in front of each of them. They were dressed in
the traditional regal purple and gold robes, and their scepters were
almost the length of their bodies. They held the metal rods with
pride, even though they were only symbolic.

The council members were placed in their positions based on
their tribe's popular vote. Gallow's Retreat had been a democracy
and safe haven for our kinds for over five decades, and even though
I didn't agree with some of the council's decisions, I understood
the reason for most of their decrees. One of them wasn't fit to rule,
however, and I was ready to challenge him.

"Corryne, born of Tribe Werewolf." My name came from a being
who had given me encouragement through my years, and I felt a
twinge of regret when I realized I had disappointed him. The feeling
passed quickly, though, as I knew my cause was greater than myself.

I acknowledged Lycon, the counselor of the werewolf Tribe. His
wise advice had always helped me, shaping my decisions indirectly.

"Are you ready to accept the conditions of your trial?"

"I am," I told him, pulling my spine as straight as my form allowed.
"But I wish to challenge the position of a tribe elder."

Any perceived offense could be eliminated with my victory against a tribal leader, and my claims against his or her rule would be justified. The counselors whispered to each other, uncertain who I would choose to battle. Only Namon and one other counselor remained silent.

Lycon was certain his conscience was clear. He remained unaffected by the murmurs around him, simply placing his hands on the sides of his podium as if he were trying to funnel his energy to me by using the podium as a conduit. Or maybe he was shattered by the decision I'd made to either rise triumphantly or die painfully from my accusation, for to call out a seasoned council member was almost always a death sentence. Only one other person had survived such a test, and he smirked at me with his thin red lips and neon green eyes.

Namon stepped from behind his podium, swiping unseen dust from his robe and striding effortlessly down the steps to meet me in the center of the room. The voices around us stopped, watching every movement for the one that would send us into battle.

Namon, counselor of the dragons, was agile and lithe, with pale skin that had never been marked by the sun. His sharp chin and jawline climbed into peaked cheekbones and a forehead with few wrinkles, even though I thought he was older than the aged elder of the werewolf tribe. He towered above me, although I was almost certain that I had recently added an inch or more to my height. He spoke to me with cold indifference, as in his mind, the battle was already won.

He didn't know my secret, though, and it had the potential to make me ten times stronger than him. All I had to do was voice my accusal, and I would prove Namon's guilt before his peers and my own.

"Say it," he challenged. "And choose your weapon wisely."

— · —

CHAPTER 1

Flick

My eyes popped open after I recognized the earthy smell of my visitor. The members of each tribe had a scent that lifted from them after a shift. I hadn't conformed to my changing body yet, but I had just as much skill as the constituents of any tribe.

I flipped Rymon over with ease. He laughed and kissed my nose before he turned me onto my back. "It wouldn't look good if my future wife could best me in battle," he chuckled.

I pushed him off me and stumbled to the bathroom. He talked to me through the door as I brushed my teeth, giving extra care to my prominent canines. I drew a thin line of black eyeliner around my eyes, extending it halfway to my temple. It made me seem older and gave more definition to my honey-brown irises.

"Are you excited?" His voice was muffled through the thick wooden door.

"About what?" I paused, holding brick-red lipstick inches from my mouth.

"We get to see it today."

I rolled my eyes when he reminded me about our field trip to see the talisman. "I saw it years ago. It wasn't that great."

He pressed his back to the door and slid down it. "My father isn't the talisman's curator, so excuse me if I'm excited."

I pressed my lips together, happy with their natural plumpness. The color I had chosen was a good contrast to my shoulder-length, coal-black hair.

"Can you pretend to be excited?"

I tossed my hair into a ponytail, allowing the thick strip of silver that ran down from my center part to remain free. "I'm excited." I mimicked his glee.

"You're lying."

I sighed. "You caught me." I tapped on the door to let him know I was coming out.

Rymon jumped up and opened the door for me, pulling the side of his mouth up in a crooked grin. The silver and blonde highlights in his chocolate-colored hair reflected the morning light. "You look beautiful."

Rymon was the most attractive werewolf of my age, and I should have swooned over his compliment. However, his exceptionally toned muscles, dark eyes, and playful remarks didn't make my heartbeat quicken. He was completely smitten with me, though.

I shook my head, letting his flattery fall around my feet. "My parents shouldn't let you come into my bedroom."

He grabbed my hand and slid his arm around my back, twirling me once across the carpet. "I've been head over heels in love with you since our third year of classes. If they thought you liked me at any point, I'd have to stay on the front porch when I came over."

I nodded along. My parents could tell I didn't have feelings for Rymon, but my choices were limited.

Several decades ago, a mermaid king came into power and tried to eliminate every race of beings who didn't align their forces with him. King Kano had already built alliances, and his reach went beyond the water. He enlisted the help of the elves and the Druids to seek out the creatures who defied his rule. The genocide resulted in the slaughter of millions. The humans who knew us as their kind thought our deaths were the result of various causes, from sicknesses and genetic defects to household falls, homicides, and travel-related accidents. In truth, we died from the things that destroyed the origin of our being. My kind were werewolves, so most of my ancestors were murdered with silver bullets.

The beings who remained gathered around the home of the magician, Archard. He cast a spell over his hometown—driving out all humans—and encasing the area in a dome. Once the invaders on the front line retreated over the rising glass structure, it closed, proving impenetrable. The refugees were safe, but it took a toll on Archard. Before he died, he used his remaining power to become a talisman. If the barrier were breached, the ruby necklace would serve as an added protection, but no one knew how to use it.

Seven tribes were formed, each one unique to the creatures it represented. My ancestors were werewolves, and we lived in the part of the town with cracker-box brick homes and meticulously manicured lawns. Other neighborhoods were designated for unicorns, trolls, faeries, dragons, griffins, and vampires.

Only thousands of our eight kinds remained, so breeding was encouraged, but only within a given species, as interbreeding would do further damage to the number of beings from a particular group. Unfortunately, the number of vampires was unchanged—since they couldn't reproduce naturally—and their bites didn't affect most of the members of the other tribes. For me, it meant one of my best friends was thrust upon me in hopes we would take vows and unite after our Glistening.

Rymon and I stepped into my living room, and the open area afforded me a glimpse of breakfast as it was prepared. My mom was making meat cakes and waffles. We didn't discuss the type of meat that graced our table, and we ate it gratefully. The animals inside the dome were limited, and the most common were deer, as the dome had been placed over a small town in southeastern North America, so I assumed a great deal of my meals comprised of venison.

My mother smiled at us as we plopped down at the table. "How hungry are you?"

Just like any other werewolf, my mother equated love with food, so she sought to stuff everyone at her table until they could hardly walk away from it. She handed us two plates full of food, and we took respectable shares.

My mother tutted me as she looked at my plate. "Only one meat cake, Corryne? You're going to starve yourself."

"I doubt it," I laughed, taking the last bite of my cake and following it with a sizable chunk of waffle.

Rymon scarfed down his breakfast before me. He waited patiently for me to finish and carried our plates to the sink. He dipped them in the dishwater and attempted to wash them before my mother playfully smacked his hands away.

"I'll take care of it. You kids need to get to school."

We grabbed our bags and walked out into the beautiful day. The weather was always pleasant under our glass shelter, thanks to the unicorns who helped control it, and several rainbows streaked across the dome. The temperature stayed mild and gentle puffs of air circulated, due to the efforts of the griffins and the trolls' underground tunnels. Don't ask me how it worked. My father explained it to me once, but my eyes glazed over before he could finish.

The dome protected us against the outside elements, even though snow would sometimes pile onto the top of it and obscure the sky for days at a time, restricting the rays that bothered the vampires and trolls. However, the dome prevented UV light from entering the town, preventing the scorching sensations that drove trolls and vampires into their dark places by day.

Rymon took my hand and ran. I allowed the touch because it was friendly and not romantic. As wolves, we were territorial creatures, and I had to shrug off most of his affections when he pressed me for a relationship, but we were still close friends.

"Look at the dome today." He stopped and turned in a full circle, staring up at the sunlight glinting off the crystalline glass.

It was usually almost clear but today blush streaks tinged its surface. *Red sky at night...* an old adage started in my mind.

It seemed like a warning.

We walked four houses down to the northwest edge of the dome. I hoped to see if it was the reflection of something that caused the sunset hue over the usually almost imperceptible structure.

The barrier between our kinds and the rest of the world was clearest at the edge. The glass-like border hummed with the force used to separate us. Regular people and the supernatural creatures who followed King Kano passed by us, oblivious to our presence.

It was one of the best views of activity beyond our isolated town. For whatever reason, humans continued to thrive and build structures within feet of our civilization. Our current view was of a beige brick fountain with shops and cafes dotted along a street that seemed to lead to the rising sun.

I was the first to notice Allistar with his hand pressed against the glass. "She's beautiful, isn't she?" he asked when he noticed us.

Allistar was my age, but he had reached the time when he was trusted to help with the inward appearance of the dome. He had been responsible for the rainbows above our head this morning.

The girl he watched was seated at one of the tables at a coffee shop. She was tall, lean, and maybe a couple of years older than me.

I felt a twinge of jealousy. I had often wondered what it would be like to feel his full lips on mine as his silvery hair fell against my face.

"It'll pass," Rymon assured him. "But you need to get your hand off the glass."

Rymon's warning was ignored as Allistar turned his attention back to the object of his fascination. Even though there was a chance he could be seen with a part of his body pressed against the glass, he watched the girl for a moment. She read a book, her legs crossed, and one hand on her chair. Her blonde hair shimmered in the sun, and I longed to feel the undiluted rays of the sun on my skin for the first time.

"If she doesn't have a boyfriend now, it won't be long before she does," Rymon said, and he clapped his hand on Allistar's back. "Once she's been deflowered, it won't be such a strong pull for you anyway."

Allistar sighed, lowering his gaze. "I wish unicorns didn't have to walk to the edges of the dome to control the weather. It's maddening to see them parading on the other side."

By *them*, he meant *human virgins*. The beings on this side of the dome weren't a problem for Allistar, but unicorns still longed for the power exuded from a human virgin beyond our borders. Some unicorns had been so rattled by the presence of virgins just beyond their reach that they had to be taken off weather detail.

"Are you guys on your way to class?" Allistar asked us.

"Yeah." Rymon stared up at the rose hues in the dome as they faded to the palest pink. "Corryne wanted to see what was causing the red tint in the dome."

Allistar gazed up into the sky. "I must not have noticed it." He gave us a sheepish grin. "I was a little busy."

I wanted to roll my eyes, but I didn't need Allistar to think I was insensitive. Or in love with him.

The guy who wanted me and the guy I wanted were so dissimilar that it was almost laughable. Rymon had almost black eyes and trim muscles, with perfect square features that made him look vulnerable and rugged at the same time. Allistar's cheekbones could cut glass, and he bore the violet eyes that marked the unicorn race. Both of them had started shifting, and their strawberry and deeply woodsy smells contrasted with one another.

Rymon put his arm around Allistar's shoulders, making the taller boy bend a little to accept his gesture. Allistar came with us willingly, but I saw him cast a look behind him.

"C'mon, lover boy," Rymon teased. "Let's get you to class before you find a way to break through the dome."

—·—

CHAPTER 2

Rymon ran ahead of us to gather some equipment for the trip. I envied the ease of his speed. I was fast, but I would be faster after the Glistening.

Allistar made easy conversation with me as we walked the last quarter of the mile to our school. We lived in a small community, so all the beings who were the same age knew each other and attended the same classes. He didn't know, though, that I had feelings for him.

"So, are you excited about your Glistening?" he asked me.

"Not really." My silver streak fell loose from behind my ear, and I pushed it back. "It's just a formality. I come from a pack of wolves, so I'll change into a wolf."

"Yeah, I guess."

I raised my eyebrows. "Do you want to be something other than a unicorn?"

He rubbed under his eyes, and a smudge from his rainbow-colored eyeliner streaked across his temple. I wanted to tell him it was there, but it exemplified his cheekbones and caused his purple-blue eyes to shine.

He noticed me watching him and chuckled. "Is everything okay?"

I wanted to stop and run my hand gently down his well-defined cheekbones. I wanted him to bring his perfectly plump lips to mine and have him take my first kiss from me as I was surrounded by his strawberry scent. Instead, I said, "You smeared your eyeliner." I motioned to his temple.

His good nature dropped, as if I had seen him naked. He wiped away most of the liner and kept running the palm of his hand over the same spot, unwilling to ask me if it was gone.

Unicorns were vain. They were born in splendid rays of the sun and aged like the sassafras albidum tree, with its green leaves turning a natural golden color before they broke away and drifted lazily to the ground. They all had shimmery silver-blonde hair, large eyes, and pale skin with strongly angular features. Everything about them was symmetrical, from the position of their widow's peak to the lengths of their limbs. Flaws were unwelcomed, and any comment that contradicted their beauty was a slight.

I had alienated him. Great. Leave it to me to make my biggest crush feel uncomfortable in the few moments I had alone with him.

"I—I'm sorry," I blubbered. "I shouldn't have said anything."

Allistar surprised me by stopping and putting his hand on my arm. "Thank you, Corryne. I'm glad you told me instead of one of the pretenders at school."

I memorized the swirling starbursts in his irises. I loved being close to him, and no one could have pulled me away from this moment.

My silver streak had gotten loose again, and he brushed it back behind my ear. I shivered, and I tried to cover it by coughing. Even though I'd looked away, it had been enough to clue Allistar into my feelings for him. He brought me around to face him, searching for my eyes when I avoided his gaze.

"It's okay," he spoke softly. "Unicorns have that effect on almost everyone."

I tried to tell him that I didn't get lost in the eyes of any other unicorn. I willed myself to say that I enjoyed his poetry and discussions about the unfairness of the Fae Wars. All I did, though, was shrug off his hands and tell him, "The sun was in my eyes."

The sun was behind me, but he didn't embarrass me by calling my attention to it. We walked in silence until the school came into view.

Before he ran inside, he jogged ahead a little, turning around to speak to me. I had never been able to jog backward, so I was impressed. He smiled, displaying his even, slightly longer teeth. "I wish things were different. I'd like to know you better."

"You've known me since we were seven years old."

"But I think I know you a little better now," he said. He threw a wink at me and turned around, disappearing into the throng of beings rushing into the school.

CHAPTER 3

Less than a thousand students roamed the halls of United Pines. Children started school at seven years old and completed their education after spending a decade there. The lower halls echoed the shrill voices of the younger children, and the teenagers roamed the rooms of the upper story.

The old brick building had once been a hospital, but our kinds didn't need a large facility for healing since most of us could heal ourselves or were almost immortal. The rooms had been easily converted into educational spaces, but there were still areas closed off from students. I tried to explore them, but I had always been caught by Namon, the leader of the dragons and biology teacher at the school.

Seven tribes of children attended classes four days a week. Vampires were absent from the building—as they couldn't add offspring to their ranks—and they didn't contribute their time to educating other beings. Their only child was over three thousand years old, and she stayed at her gothic-styled home, looking out the top window with almost unblinking eyes.

"Hey," Rymon called after me. "I got it." He held up the recording device.

"Will the elders let you record our trip?"

He shrugged. "I probably won't be able to film the amulet, but I can chronicle the rest of the trip."

I was glad he was carrying the equipment through the halls. He usually tried to touch me in some way—now that he was certain our vows were pending—but his heavy load would prevent him from creating the illusion that we were a couple.

We checked into the office, and Bara, the griffin who organized the electronic files corresponding to the staff and students, barely regarded us. We pressed our fingerprints onto a screen and hurried outside, hoping we hadn't missed our transportation.

Our class fringed on adulthood, so we were given more freedom than the other groups. We weren't herded by our teachers from one place to the next, but the penalties were high if we misbehaved.

We loaded onto a gray-green bus that had once been used to transport people who violated human laws. It smelled like the old lockers in the school and the hamper after my father had added a couple of pairs of his socks to it.

Rymon nudged me into a seat, and he squeezed next to me. "Hard to believe they're taking all forty of us, huh?"

I shrugged. "It's not really that big of a group, and we're almost adults."

He sucked in a laugh and let it bray out his mouth. "Bah! Have you paid attention to the kids that are in our Glistening year? All of us are troublemakers!"

I pursed my lips. "Not all of us."

He raised his eyebrows. It was clear he thought I was referencing myself.

I rolled my eyes. "Obviously, not me, but what about Allistar and Fiona?"

Rymon flashed his digital camera, an ancient device that still worked, and adjusted the settings. "We just pulled Allistar away from the barrier, and Fiona is a fayrie. She's just like her sister."

As if on cue, Fiona and her sister, Fallyn, plopped onto the seat in front of us. Fallyn turned around, flipping her long, intricately braided black ponytail over her shoulder. Her coffee-colored skin was dewy and unblemished, with a soft, golden glow across her cheeks and down her arms. "Can't you feel it?" she asked. "The power of the amulet is stronger today."

"I think it's weaker," Fiona contradicted.

Fallyn spoke over her sister's words. "I think it's going to choose one of us."

"For what?" Rymon and I spoke together.

Fiona turned around in her seat—a mirror of her sister's features—but manipulated them into a different expression. "Don't tell me that you've never heard the story?"

Allistar slipped into the seat behind us with his girlfriend, Felicity. Their scents almost overwhelmed me. The faerie's smell was easier; it was woodsy, a lot like mine.

Fiona was waiting for my response, and some words tumbled out of my mouth. "I know there's some sort of prophecy, but I doubt it involves our generation."

Felicity giggled at something Allistar said, and I was momentarily distracted. I tried to hear a swatch of their conversation. Part of Felicity's soft, porcelain face was reflected in my window. Her hair had been trimmed into a soft chin-length style, and her cheeks blushed with the perfect amount of color.

"Are you even listening?" Fallyn asked.

"I'm sorry. What did you say?"

Fiona took a deep breath and politely repeated herself. "A darkened heart will bring light. An act of friendship will set everything right."

Rymon smirked. "Speaking of a darkened heart."

I followed his gaze. Zaffron and two other dragons boarded the bus and sneered at the beings startled by their commanding presence. Their long, black coats and black eyeliner made them appear more menacing.

Two fayries with ivory skin, slanted eyes, and mischievous green eyes fell into the seat on top of Fallyn and Fiona. They sat on their laps, even though the girls resisted.

"You're incorrigible!" Fiona cried.

"And you'll get to give me the keys to your eternal heart," Puck replied from atop her lap, mocking the words from traditional vows of a union.

"Ugh! Only if you live until the Glistening," she warned.

Patt, Puck's identical brother, wriggled on Fallyn's lap. She grimaced but put her arms around his waist.

Zaffron, surrounded by his usual group of followers, scoffed at them. "Why were so many fayries born the same year as me?"

Puck smiled up at them. "We can't help it if your parents can only have one little lizard a cycle, but our kind can have multiples."

Zaffron grabbed his collar and lifted him off his girlfriend's lap. Patt stayed frozen, unwilling to be caught in the crossfire.

"One more word, and I'll rip your wings off." His threat was empty, but we all knew he would hurt Puck if the fayrie continued to mock him.

"He's had enough," Rymon spoke up. His voice was firm and unwavering. I could feel his nerves on edge, but his face reflected no distress. I was proud of my friend for standing up to a dragon, especially when the odds weren't in his favor. Despite his reputation for fighting anyone who opposed him, Zaffron was almost a foot taller than Rymon.

Zaffron eyeballed Rymon without letting go of Puck. "Why should I listen to a dog?" He released Puck so forcefully that he bumped into Fiona, taking her breath. "You'll just run away with your tail tucked between your legs."

Rymon jumped out of his seat. I grabbed his camera before it fell. "Do you want to find out?"

Red-hot anger radiated off him. I felt the pull to stand with him, but I pushed it down. My feelings of loyalty to a member of my tribe were instinctual, but they would hurt the situation more than help it.

Allistar intervened, standing up and putting a hand on each boy's chest. "Hey, guys. We all want to see the talisman, so can we calm down before the elders decide to take away the privilege?"

"Sure," Zaffron agreed. His eyes flicked to me. "I wouldn't want to embarrass him in front of his girlfriend."

Rymon started to jump at him again, but Allistar put an arm around him in a brotherly motion. Rymon shrugged it off but sat back down.

"You know he could incinerate you," Patt said after Zaffron and his goons had taken seats at the back of the bus.

"Not yet," Rymon responded, rotating his shoulders to move his clothes into a more comfortable position. "Dragons can't breathe fire until after their Glistening."

"Still, I've seen his colors after a shift," Fiona revealed. "He's going to be terrifying."

"I'm not scared of him," Rymon asserted.

"Of course not," Fallyn piped up, rolling her eyes.

He stared at her, willing her to speak against him again. I put my hand on his arm. He was my best friend, and I knew how to calm him. My touch soothed his bruised ego, and he took the digital camera from me.

I wasn't prepared when he snapped a picture of me. I pleaded with him to erase it, but he wouldn't listen to my protests. "You don't know how beautiful you are."

"I say that to her all the time," Fallyn called back to us. Patt was still firmly on her lap, so she couldn't twist in the seat.

I offered up a lame defense. "I'm short, and I have brown eyes."

All the fayries in front of us laughed, and Fiona declared, "Brown eyes can be beautiful, and yours look like they've been mixed with honey."

Puck hopped off Fiona's lap. "Girly stuff is boring." He pulled his mouth down in the corners in an expression of mock sadness. "Let's go float the trolls' clubs over their heads."

Patt eyed him mischievously. "Let's do it."

They were gone before I could protest. "Why don't they leave them alone?"

Free from the pressure of her boyfriend's weight, Fallyn turned around. "They like to play around. They don't call them names or threaten them."

My friend was referencing our recent run-in with Zaffron. I decided to turn it around on her. "What they're doing is just as bad. Those poor Trolls don't know what's happening until they see their clubs over their heads."

Already, Puck and Patt sniggered behind the seat of two trolls, Bredek and Amos. Their clubs were suspended over their heads by faerie magic while they looked for them in their seat and under it.

Puck and Patt high-fived each other. I stood up and marched to the trolls' seats, knocking the chuckling offenders on the back of their heads.

"What's wrong with you?" I yelled down at them, my hand on my hip.

I grabbed the first club, and I had a moment where I was afraid that the club would resist my force, but the magic was released. I took both clubs in my hands and gave them back to their owners. The trolls hung their heads when they thanked me, and my heart went out to them.

"It's not your fault," I said loudly. "Sometimes fayrie magic should stay in the dark."

The teenagers on the bus quietened. I had spoken part of a well-known binding spell.

"That's enough." The voice was firm and unfeeling. Namon the Impaler, the dragon leader on the council and one of our professors, stood before me. "What are you doing out of your seat?"

It was one thing to chastise Puck and Patt in front of the kids in our class, but I didn't want to get them in trouble with an elder. I faced Namon and said nothing.

Dragons didn't like for any being to hold their eyes. Still, I didn't back down, and everyone witnessed my defiance. Without breaking eye contact, Namon ordered me to sit with the dragons. "Your race knows fear, girl. We do not." His self-satisfied smile was thin and brief.

I walked to the back of the bus with my head held high. I surveyed my three options before I sat down. All three dragons in my class had their own seat. No one wanted to sit with them, and they didn't want to crowd their egos by sitting with each other.

Mantible stared at me, daring me to meet his gaze, widening his small, bottle-green eyes. I passed his seat and had to choose between the dragons at the rear-most part of the bus. Nava was the obvious choice since we were both females, but instead, I chose the dragon that everyone considered the meanest. I slid into the seat beside Zaffron.

Surprise registered on his features. He stared straight forward, and when the bus started to move, he closed his eyes as if he was uncomfortable with the feeling of bouncing down the old road. His face paled once, but he didn't open his eyes.

My friends stared back at me sympathetically. Puck and Patt raised the hair on the back of the trolls' mullets. I could feel the heat coming off me, and that's when I noticed I had Zaffron's attention.

He opened his mouth in a yawn and sent two purple sparks flying toward the middle of the bus. They hit their marks, and Puck and Patt jumped out of their seats from the shock.

"Thank you," I told him. At the sound of my voice, Zaffron sighed heavily and looked out the window, as if talking to me were beneath him.

When we arrived, I jumped out of my seat and almost ran to my friends. Fallyn bombarded me with questions when we stepped off the bus. "What was it like back there? Could you feel the heat off him? Did you tell him to shoot sparks at Puck and Patt?" She was excited, and I had to remind her to lower her voice, as the dragons were only ten feet away.

"Hey! We were the ones who got shot!" Puck and Patt exclaimed together.

Fallyn waved their outrage away. "You didn't feel more than a little electric shock. I could have felt the same thing if I had shuffled across the carpet and touched a metal doorknob."

We were called into one large group, and I was saved from answering any of Fallyn's questions. Allistar stood on the other side of me, and Felicity took his hand. Rymon tried to hold my hand, but I moved it to fix my ponytail.

As the elders went over the rules, I watched Felicity out of the corner of my eye. I wanted to hate her since I had a crush on her boyfriend, but she was nice, and she smiled at me when she saw me staring at her. I waved my hand and looked forward, the fires of embarrassment rising from my chest and coloring my face.

Felicity was certain she'd be taking vows with Allistar after this year's Glistening. He hadn't officially asked her to be his mate or visited her parents for their blessing, but it was assumed they would take vows since they were the only two unicorns left in our year.

How would she feel if she knew about the human Allistar had watched this morning? Would she be angry, or would she have watched her as well? Unicorns had a strong pull to human virgins, and it was likely that Felicity wouldn't have been immune to the human's charms.

The professors who had chosen to take us, divided our class into three groups. Most of the trolls were in Zahava's group. Her ebony hair flashed sunlight as she gathered them together. She spoke her expectations loudly and firmly, and the trolls followed her without a grumbled complaint.

The rest of us were divided between Aella and Namon. I hoped I would be chosen for Aella's group. She had picked all the griffins, though, and that left little room in her group. She called Fiona's and Felicity's names, and they ran to join her. Aella's bright orange and yellow feathers ruffled when she entered the cool cave, but they settled, offering her a blanket of protection.

I had always marveled at the appearance of the griffins. They never fully resumed a human form after they walked under the Glistening tree. The flesh on their noses almost curved into a beak, their eyes became almost beady, and their plumage remained on their arms and torsos. They had used a glamor to live among the humans, and the humans had never guessed their difference. Mortals were oblivious to their soft, wintery scent, like snowflakes rushing to your face after a frigid breeze.

"The rest of you will follow me." Namon barked his command at us. "Each of you has proven to be the most troublesome out of your year, but I will not give in to your hijinks" —his gaze settled on Puck— "or varied excuses." His eyes shifted to me. Without another word, he turned on his heel and ducked into the cave's entrance.

The caves were chilly, but the warm blood of my wolf nature kept me from feeling cold. We wound through the well-worn trail of dirt, with stalagmites and stalactites on either side of us.

Most of the fayries, werewolves, and dragons stayed in their own small groups. Rymon and I seemed to attract the leftovers. Patt, Puck, and Fallyn were the first to join us, I invited Bredek when I saw he was alone and unsure of himself, and Rymon motioned Allistar over.

"You're a troublemaker," Rymon mused when Allistar sidled up to him.

"Yeah, Professor Namon must have heard me when I tried to keep his son from beating up Puck." He playfully punched Puck in the arm. The fayrie rubbed the place on his arm, but Allistar didn't notice.

"Oh, yeah. It wasn't because you were looking at a human at the border." Rymon rested his hands on his chin and blinked rapidly. I laughed at his playfully lovestruck face.

"You were drawn to a human!" Fallyn exclaimed. Her outburst got the attention of several werewolves, and she lowered her voice. "I didn't think you were allowed to get that close to the populated parts of the barrier."

"I didn't try to tear through the dome to get to her," Allistar defended.

"But you might have if Corryne and I hadn't been there." Rymon cut in.

Allistar shook his head. "I've never done it before," he admitted. His eyes widened when he realized what he'd revealed.

Fallyn was as serious as I had ever seen her. She placed her hand on his arm. "How many times have you watched the same human?"

"Two or three times."

We all let out a sigh of relief. Bredek didn't join us. Instead, he added, "In the last two days."

My eyes darted to him. His hefty frame struggled to keep up with us, and his dark gray skin was ashen. We let everyone else pass our little group, so it was easier for him to match our pace.

We waited for clarification. Trolls weren't athletic creatures, so it took him a few moments to regain his composure. Allistar stared daggers at him, but the troll was unaffected. Their demeanor was innocent, and it left no room for lies or deception. When Bredek caught his breath he told us, "The unicorn watches Miriam from the border. I can see him from my house."

Fallyn slapped Allistar's arm. "What are you thinking?"

The rest of us were flabbergasted while we watched the exchange between the three of them. We had fallen behind our main group, but they were still in sight.

"Wait!" Fallyn rounded on Bredek. "How do you know her name is Miriam?"

Allistar opened his mouth to lie, but Fallyn put her finger on his lips. She gave Bredek her full attention, coaxing the troll to speak again.

He shrugged his shoulders. "She told him."

We all gasped.

"You let her see you through the barrier?" I didn't realize I had spoken until Allistar glared at me.

"I don't have to explain myself to you," he spat.

I was instantly defensive. "Then maybe you'd like to tell the council!" I threw as much venom as possible into my words. "What did you do, shift and touch the barrier with your horn?" His speechlessness confirmed my accusation and fueled my fire. "Great! Why don't you just open it up for her and let her bring King Kano's army with her!"

My anger could be explained by the need for secrecy, but my threat was excessive. It made me sound like a scorned lover instead of a caring friend.

Two fayries, Breeze and Crisp, had been hiding behind a large rock and listening to us. When they were recognized, they bolted back to the group.

"They're going to tell," Puck said, and Patt nodded.

Allistar snorted and stormed off, shrugging away our whispered apologies.

We hurried to catch up to the main group, and I spotted Namon. Breeze and Crisp hadn't reached him with the news of Allistar's offence yet, and he stood with his arms crossed, his usual sneer pasted across his face.

Aella spoke to the gathered creatures outside the talisman's chamber. We had missed the history that involved King Kano's rising and the resulting genocide, but she was only getting started.

Griffins had protected the Glistening Tree before Archard's spell. They made rounds to check on its stability, but they usually left it alone. No one in our borders wanted to hurt it. Deforestation had been the only reason our kinds had set up a patrol around the tree in the outside world, and we respected our oxygen-giving plants, so unnecessary logging practices were absent from our communities.

In addition to monitoring the Glistening Tree, the griffins oversaw the historical and genealogical records for our kinds and policed our town. They took their positions seriously, and most of their young could recite oral traditions and laws by the time they entered school.

Aella waved her arms as she spoke, and the firelight danced across her brilliant feathers, making them look like a moving sunset. "When my grandfather, Artemis, came here, he begged for Archard's help. Archard was the most powerful wizard of his age, but he realized that the spell he would cast could end his life. Heroically, he placed his remaining energy into his sister's ruby necklace."

"I thought it was his *wife's* necklace," Nava commented.

Aella didn't chastise her for speaking up. She enjoyed healthy discussions with her students. "As you may remember from your lessons, Archard did not take a wife."

The class collectively murmured their agreement.

Aella went on with her explanation. "Archard's essence transferred into the necklace, making it a talisman that supplied our races with a small protection if King Kano ever breached the barriers."

"Isn't he dead yet?" Mantible called out. He laughed and looked at Zaffron to join him, but Zaffron stood with his arms crossed, indifferent.

Aella's voice took on lower tones, and her bright expression clouded over. "We should never speak so flippantly about mortality." She walked up to him, calling everyone's attention to the tactlessness of his comment. "The mermaid king has outlived two generations of griffins and will likely continue to rule past the reign of my daughter."

Some griffin males had defining roles, like Aella's grandfather, but their culture was matriarchal. Aella was on the council because she was considered the ruler of her people. When she passed away, her daughter, Anila, would be the primary keeper of the oral traditions of the creatures under Archard's dome.

Anila's Glistening was several years away, but her brother, Talon, was in our class. He sat on the ground with his back against a cave wall. His girlfriend, Hana, shared a seed bar with him. He was one of the most apathetic learners in our year. His family held status among his kind, but he wasn't expected to rule, so he glided through his classes, barely passing any of them. He had been smart when we were young, but by his second or third year in classes, he understood that his mother wasn't going to choose him as her successor.

Aella stared at Mantible until he looked away. She turned around and he snarled.

Namon had wound his way around the crowd of students, and he stood behind us. I could feel his warm breath on my neck, and I smelled soot, the scent of his kind.

We were hyperaware of Namon's presence as we filtered into the chamber. Even Bredek kept his club close to his body for comfort. Namon could turn us all to ash with one fiery breath. He wouldn't do it during a class trip, but we were still aware of his incendiary power.

My dad passed us on his way out. He was only a little taller than me with the same dark eyes and hair. He nodded to me, but it was only a casual acknowledgment. Werewolves were not overly affectionate with their young. Cubs were loved, but neither parent coddled them.

I could hear the amulet before I saw it. A buzz rushed to my ears and materialized in the form of vibrating reds and oranges.

In front of me, a bright red glow thumped like a heartbeat, but the light seemed dimmer than it had on the day my dad had brought me to work with him.

Whispered voices circled around me, but I couldn't focus on more than their sound. The words escaped me, but the voices were diverse and plentiful. Before I knew it, I was on the ground. Allistar and Rymon hovered above my head, and each wore a look of concern.

"What's wrong?" Rymon asked me.

I sat up and rubbed my head, my temples throbbing. "How long was I out?"

"Just a minute," Allistar answered.

Rymon took off his hoodie and handed it to me. "Put it on. You're cold as ice."

I slipped it over my head, and some red lipstick rubbed against the collar. I turned out the collar and showed Rymon the stain, but he shook his head at my apology.

"What else can I do to help?" Rymon liked to feel useful, and he hated to see me distressed.

"The pup needs to get up," Namon ordered.

In Namon's prime, werewolves were referred to as "dogs." Under Archard's dome, we had united over the years, and some words were seen as derogatory now.

Blood rushed to my face. As much as I despised Naman and his prejudices, I had to remain calm. My actions would reflect on my father's parenting, and he needed to keep his job.

Rymon looked up to defend me, but I stopped him. "Can you help me get up?"

Distracted by my request, my friend instantly complied, gently lifting me onto my feet. I had only accepted his assistance to keep him from upsetting Namon, and I let go of his arm as soon as Namon's attention was diverted.

"What happened?" Fallyn asked. "I can sprinkle some dust over you if you want. It'll help if you forgot to eat this morning."

"I don't need fayrie magic," I barked. Fallyn raised her eyebrows, and I apologized. "I don't know what happened."

I allowed Rymon to lead me to our group. His hands were tight on my hips, and they felt more restrictive than helpful.

Our class had surrounded the talisman, and our circle was wide enough to allow everyone an unobstructed view. No one was immune to the pull of the bright red ruby. It could enchant us in a way beyond any other being's individual power.

The talisman lay casually on a rock as if its owner had simply placed it there so they could take a swim in the nearby stream. Its simple chain and setting reflected a brightness, even though there was no natural light in the room. The ruby borrowed the gleam from the setting and chain, coloring the stone like crimson blood around the edges and pooling into a maroon center.

My father reappeared. He stepped to the middle of the circle and stared at the necklace reverently. He steepled his fingers before he spoke. "Good morning." His voice betrayed a slight accent that many people associated with the lower part of the western hemisphere. The class was silent as they waited for his presentation.

"The talisman hangs from a cable chain with a lobster clasp," he intoned proudly, delivering his words with a crispness that bounced against the walls of the inner chamber. "The one-inch, or two and fifty-four hundredths centimeters, ruby is held in place by a fixed bail setting comprised of a yellow and white gold mixture. The ruby itself was mined in nearby North Carolina." He paused for the other students to whisper in disbelief.

I had heard his speech about the necklace many times. He practiced it in front of my mother and me, adding new tidbits that he hardly ever inserted into the talk he gave during every tour. I was proud of my father's devotion to the talisman. He was its trusted curator, but since he also cleaned the caves after tours, he was simply seen as a custodian.

A rush of questions flew from my classmates. Aella and Zahava moved their hands from their shoulders to their mid-waists, gesturing at their students to lower their volumes. Namon glared at our group, and everyone around me quieted.

"You can speak," Zahava told a troll to her left.

The troll put her hand down and glanced around shyly. "Do you ever pick it up and clean it?"

Zahava put her head in her hand, embarrassed over the question the troll from her group had asked. One of our first lessons taught us about the creatures who had tried to touch the talisman. It had appeared in the cave, and it had remained there. It emitted a green glow when it was touched, and the beings who touched it either died or went into a deep coma. Even vampires were leery of its defensive magic.

"No," my father answered with a benign smile.

Fallyn raised her hand. Namon noticed her, but it took a moment before he sighed heavily and acknowledged her attempt to ask my father a question.

"The fayrie wishes to speak," he said. Fallyn opened her mouth, but Namon added, "As if we weren't already shamed by the troll's question."

The troll who had spoken to my father cried into her hands. Her friends, male and female trolls, gathered around her protectively while she wept.

Fallyn's voice came out squeaky at first but became more confident. "Does Archard ever try to communicate with you?"

My father had sometimes heard a high-pitched ringing coming from the necklace, but he stopped speaking about it after my mother and the council members couldn't hear it.

"No," he lied. "I hear nothing but the wind through the caves."

"Are the caves haunted?" Talon piped up. A sharp look from his mother only made him smile mischievously.

My father barely acknowledged his question. It was clear that our class was one of the hardest he'd had to endure. "There are no ghosts of which I am aware."

My father didn't believe in spirits. I had a differing opinion, and I thought there were many haunted possibilities within the dome.

Namon clapped his hands once, and we were startled to attention. "Okay, pay your respects to the talisman and get out." He spun on his heel, going down a tunnel to the left.

Aella stared after him. "That was rather abrupt, but Professor Namon is right. We need to get back to the school by lunchtime."

Each of my classmates walked up to the talisman and stared at it for a moment. No one was truly impressed by it except for Rymon and Fiona. Rymon tried to snap a picture of it, but my father grabbed the camera out of his hands as he was lining up for a shot.

Fiona took the longest. It was like she was trying to gather strength from the crimson ruby's core. Aella led her away as she reluctantly stared back at the talisman. She seemed transfixed by it.

In the first years under the dome's protection, there had been a religious cult of creatures who idolized the necklace. To my father's dismay, some of them included werewolves. He had to set up extra defense details, relying on the help of the vampires, Sitali and Ledot, a mother and daughter who ruled their kind together. Finally, the cult disbanded after several members died when they touched the necklace.

Zahava put her hand on my shoulder. "It is your turn."

I was as close to the talisman as my feet would comfortably carry me. "I can visit it anytime." I didn't try to lie and say that I had already had my turn. Trolls were known for their infallible memories.

Zahava smiled sweetly and led me to the rock on which the necklace was displayed. I held back, and she pulled me. "It is your turn," she repeated kindly but firmly.

The buzzing entered my mind like bees in a hive. I shook my head once to try to clear it, but the sound intensified until it invaded my head, vibrating my face and blurring my vision.

I looked back at my friends for help, but Rymon only raised his eyebrows, and Fallyn moved her hands in a shooing gesture. They didn't understand the reason for my hesitation, and I wasn't sure that I could string the words together to share it with them. Bredek stared at me and tilted his head, and Allistar wandered away from our group. Earlier, I had seen him with Breeze and Crisp, trying to talk them out of reporting him.

"It is beautiful, no?" Zahava asked me.

The fires in the torches mounted on the cave walls flickered. They made shadows that danced demons on the walls.

I could hardly hear her over my pounding brain. "No. I mean, yes. Can I go now?"

The light from the fires wavered, causing shapes to grow large and small on the cave walls. The talking turned into muted chatter, but I couldn't make out any words. I was focused on trying not to pass out again.

My vision darkened around the edges until the only thing I could see was the necklace on the rock. The maroon appeared to pool over the crimson around it in beats, just like a heart. I almost thought I saw the shape of an eye in the center of the ruby, forming into an iris and melting into blood.

Then the fires went out.

— · —

CHAPTER 4

It was complete pandemonium. Students screamed, and feet pounded the earth. I was aware of their blind steps as they tripped over my limbs. My father's scent wafted to me, and he lifted me off the floor of the cave. I didn't remember falling or passing out, but I could have lost consciousness in the darkness.

A bright blue flame cut through the darkness, and I lifted my head to see its source. Namon stood with his arms spread, maintaining the blaze by blowing from his lips instead of the back of his throat. It was rumored that a dragon's eternal flame remained ignited in his or her belly and spewed forth with only a breath.

"Is she okay?"

I was started by the smell of ash. My father nodded to Zaffron. Rymon helped my father lift me to my feet as Zaffron, Mantible, and Nava lit the torches on the wall. Mantible only ignited one torch; he hadn't fully adjusted to his shifting body.

There was a hiss and a pop when Namon stopped blowing his flame. He had run back when he had heard the chaos, and I was glad for his quick thinking until he spoke. "Unacceptable." His leering voice echoed off the wall, chastising each one of us. "Are you rats afraid of the dark?" He scrutinized each one of us. I shrugged off Rymon's hand on my arm, but not before Namon saw my weakness and judged me. "We *are* the reason humans fear the dark. Have we lived here in this" —he searched for the right word— "*bubble* so long that our children scatter like bugs in the light?"

Zaffron leaned against the wall, the sole of one foot resting against it. He motioned to Mantible, Nava, and himself. "We were standing erect when the—"

"Insubordination!" Namon yelled at his son.

Zaffron lowered his eyes. Dragons were like werewolves; under-lings submitted to their alpha.

"I will speak plainly so your delicate minds will hear my words," Namon went on. "You will follow me to the bus." A spark of fire threatened in his eyes, and his voice dropped into a slow hiss, seething out the words. "You will sit quietly until we arrive at the school, and you will not test me again."

Everyone in his group followed him with their heads down. Fallyn kept glancing at me, but I didn't acknowledge her attempts to whis-per before we got to the bus.

When we were loading, Rymon scooted me toward the seat we had occupied, but Namon stopped him with one word. "No." He pointed at the back of the bus.

I rejoined Zaffron. At one point during the ride back, I felt sorry for him. It must have been hard for him to have grown up under Namon's rigid rule. I only had to endure it at school, but he had to deal with stiff words and rigid expectations all the time. He didn't look at me. He stared straight ahead, registering the movement around him without expression.

I shuffled inside the school with my peers. Namon went to his office as soon as we returned, his black robes billowing behind him as he walked. We didn't see him for the rest of the day, and no one complained about his absence.

Our class ate lunch in dispirited silence, and Zahava and Aella mirrored our glum expressions. Zaffron was at the recycler when I approached it, scraping almost all his lunch into it.

Maybe it was the sad look on his face or his dejected movements that caused me to speak to him. "Thank you for checking on me after the fires blew out."

At first, I didn't think he heard me. After a moment, he dutifully replied, "You were part of my group."

Dragons shared a quality with my kind. Both dragons and were-wolves were fiercely loyal. During the time I had been included in his father's group, Zaffron had felt responsible for me. I had foolishly mistaken his interest in my well-being as a sign that he was open to friendship.

I stepped back, almost feeling chastened, even though Zaffron hadn't been rude. Dragons and werewolves weren't known for sentimentality. Yet, I had hoped for a budding camaraderie.

"Why were you talking to him?" Rymon asked me when I got back to our table. His jaw clenched and unclenched, and color brushed his cheeks.

I answered him honestly, amused by his jealousy. "I thanked him for checking on me."

"I checked on you, too."

Fiona and Fallyn pretended to look through their shoulder bags. Bredek had stayed with our group when we came back to school, and he shoveled large handfuls of food into his mouth, pretending he didn't hear the conversation.

Rymon stared at me, waiting on an answer to a question he didn't ask. Finally, he gave up. "Why did you thank him, but you never consider anything I do for you?"

I tried to laugh so my friends would feel more at ease. "Thanks for helping me."

He scoffed and crossed his arms. "I hope you aren't like this after we say our vows."

My head jerked so fast that it should have spun off my neck. Our parents had always assumed Rymon and I would take vows after our Glistenings, but we had never really discussed it, especially in front of our friends. I could feel the heat rise from my chest to my neck.

"And I hope you won't be a jealous jerk who tries to control everything I do," I shot at him.

The gloves were off, and our friends were stuck in place as we stared at each other. Out of the corner of my eye, I could see Fiona staring at us, frozen, too nervous to continue pretending she was rummaging through her bag.

"Lovers spat?" Allistar playfully punched Rymon's arm.

Thankfully, Rymon didn't answer him.

Fiona nudged Allistar with her elbow. "Where were you?"

He took an apple off her tray and bit into it. "I was trying to talk Crisp and Breeze out of reporting me."

"Did it work?" I asked.

He continued to chew, ignoring my question. Fiona looked from Allistar to me, trying to figure out what had happened between us.

"They'll report you," Fallyn confirmed. "They'll see what they can get from you for their silence first, but they'll tell."

Allistar paused, a bite of the apple in his mouth. "I offered them my first wish."

"You what?" Rymon's eyebrows furrowed. "I thought you were supposed to save that for Felicity."

The first wish a unicorn bestowed with their horn was the most significant. The wish could cross the bounds of time and space, sometimes bringing others back from the brink of death. A unicorn usually gave his or her first wish to their betrothed after their Glistening. It was a sign of their commitment to the other unicorn.

Allistar waved Rymon's question away. "If they tell on me, it won't matter who I give my first wish. Namon will have his foot on my neck."

"He would love that," Fallyn commented.

Dragons thought they were superior to all other beings, but they had a particular disdain for unicorns and fayries. Even Fiona, who was studious and congenial, suffered when Namon's watchful eye fell on her.

"What can I do to stop them?" Bits of apple landed on the table in front of him as he spoke.

Fallyn shrugged. "There's nothing you can do. They're my neighbors, and they spy on my house all the time."

Fiona spoke up. "They told on us for sneaking in a pet rat."

"But we didn't say anything when they put scorch marks on their ceiling and borrowed white toothpaste from us to cover it up." Fallyn dropped her fork onto her tray like she had delivered the last word in an argument.

"They put scorch marks on their ceiling?" I asked.

Fallyn nodded, finally removing her hand from her bag as the tension around the table lessened. "They made their fireworks and thought it'd be a good idea to set them off inside their house."

"They had to know that wouldn't end well," Rymon said.

"They're not very smart," Fallyn agreed.

Fiona raised her index finger like she was trying to raise her hand during a classroom discussion. "That's not fair. I think the mechanics behind developing fireworks shows that the boys are smart. Their parents aren't home a lot, so they seem to act out to get attention."

Allistar put his half-eaten apple back on Fiona's tray. "I'll just have to charm them."

Fallyn rolled her eyes. "You think you have the power to charm fayries?"

He spread his hands wide, directing us to look at his near-perfect form.

Fallyn giggled. "That may work on other unicorns, but I don't think your good looks will keep Breeze and Crisp from reporting you."

I was a little irked by my friend's insinuation. "Other kinds could find him attractive. We aren't glued to our ancestors' strict rules against interspecies mating."

"Actually, we are," Rymon interjected, putting his arm around my shoulder. "Our kinds would completely diminish in numbers if we allowed intermarrying between the beings under the dome."

I shrugged off his arm. "You sound just like our parents."

I registered the wounded look on his face before he shrugged and took his tray to the recycler. He didn't think there was anything wrong with what he'd said, and that made him part of the problem.

Puck and Patt attempted to lighten the mood by staring at Allistar with faraway eyes. "You *are* dreamy," they joked.

Everyone at the table laughed, and my mind flashed to my earlier exchange with Allistar. Sure, he was upset with me now, but there was a moment that morning—with the sun shining a sparkle into his eyes—when I wondered if he liked me.

I shook my head to clear my thoughts, but my eyes wandered back to Allistar. Even though he seemed irritated with me, I thought I saw his gaze linger a little longer in my direction.

I resisted the urge to look after him when he left the table. There was no way a werewolf and a unicorn could be together. Because if there was, I'd practically tear the dome down to find it.

—•—

CHAPTER 5

"I've been fired."

My mother and I looked up from our candy meat stew. She put her hand on my father's arm, but I could only stare at him.

My father had been distant when he came home from work. We had heard his car rumble into the garage, but he hadn't entered the house for some time. When he had emerged, he had looked defeated and anxious.

He'd opened the door and marched straight to the bathroom. My mother lowered her dark eyes and continued preparing dinner. I tried to press her to see if she had any clue about the reason for my father's strange behavior, but she remained silent.

My father buried his face in his hands. "It's been thirty-five years. Everything I know is about that necklace."

"I'm so sorry," my mother consoled him. She stood up and hugged him, accidentally covering his face in a blanket of her thick, black hair.

He smiled up at her gratefully. Their eyes locked, and years of happiness and challenges passed between them.

"Is it because of me?"

My father seemed surprised by my question. "No, Corryne." His brows furrowed as he considered whether he should reveal the reason for his dismissal. "The ruby has dimmed."

"What's that mean?" I asked.

He leaned back in his chair, and my mother returned to her seat. "I wish it meant nothing, but I can already tell there is a difference in the caves." He took the napkin off his lap and folded it several times. "Animals started wandering in from the forest. They usually stay just beyond the border."

The griffins had set up a border around the cave using the power in their feathers. It was unseen, but it seemed to repel any creature or being from entering the area within two hundred feet of the necklace. A small entryway was left untouched, and the curator, a dragon, or a vampire guarded it carefully.

His explanation left me with more questions.

"Will the dome still work?

"What's going to happen now?

"Who's watching the caves in your place?"

He held his hand up. "The vampires have been called upon to choose a worker from their ranks. The council hopes it will keep the animals out of the caves if they sense the presence of a predator there."

"You went before the council?" The words were out of my mouth before I could stop them. My father had been assigned a job by the council, so, of course, they had convened to terminate it.

"I think that's enough, Corryne," my mother cautioned.

"It's okay, Maureen. She's been carried away by the excitement today." He placed his napkin beside his untouched bowl of stew. "I think I'll retire early tonight. I'll feel better after I sleep."

My mother dutifully followed him to attend to his bedtime preparations. I imagined being subservient to Rymon, and it made me sick. *Could I shave him and bathe him each day?* It sounded silly to the other beings who lived here, but in our culture, it was one of the ways a wife showed appreciation to her husband.

My father was a good man, but why did my mother sacrifice her dreams, pride, and autonomy to be considered a good wife? She wasn't even allowed to drive, for Archard's sake!

I washed the dishes and climbed the steps to my room. I heard my name and inched closer to my parent's closed bedroom door. Muffled patches of conversation echoed into the hallway, but only a few sentences came through clearly.

"It was just like the last time she was there." My father spoke in a hushed tone.

Their words became too quiet to hear, and I almost gave up when he said, "The council thinks the barrier is weakening, and with the power of the necklace draining, we won't have any protection at all."

CHAPTER 6

To me, werewolf biology was cut and dry. We could run fast, smell the notes of every essence, and after we walked under the Glistening Tree, we could transform into beasts that could rip apart a mortal man in seconds. Werewolf reproduction was a little harder to wrap my head around.

A new couple could conceive offspring within months of their union, but they had to wait decades before another child was possible. Often, a subsequent cub would be raised alongside a niece or nephew in much the same way as humans have cousins.

My brother, Hamlet, was eighteen years older than me. To our father's dismay, he rejected the curator's position and chose to work with griffins in the dome's small police force.

Hamlet visited our house every Sunday, dutifully filling the spaces that were empty in his absence. Our mother was especially pleased to see him. Even though he arrived like clockwork every Sunday, she'd pull him into a hug and exclaim, "I'm so glad you could visit us this week!"

My brother was apathetic to her attention, only making required appreciative remarks. Still, he was celebrated like a returning war hero every week.

He was old enough to be my father, but he seemed both older and younger than his years. He often appeared at the house with a stubbly chin and dark oily hair, smelling like sweat and day-old pizza. In his youth, the other werewolves his age had called him "Ham" because of his rounded middle, and he hated the nickname. He lacked the maturity to properly maintain his appearance, and he liked to spread gossip about the community members who called the station for help.

I used to idolize him when I was young. He once pulled me away from the road sharply when I had wandered too close to the curb, and I suffered from some serious hero worship. I thought my brother loved me and cared about my life and well-being. In truth, he was only trying to keep me from a certain death.

The difference between what I thought he felt and his actual intentions became clear to me when I tried to crawl into his lap several weeks after he'd saved my life. He had pushed me off brusquely without saying a word. Our mother had picked me up, placing me on her hip.

He must have thought I was too young to remember or understand him, because he said, "You need to keep a better eye on your whelp, Mother." Even though I was a little better than a toddler, I recalled his words, and I have hardly spoken to him since.

My mother and father were getting older, and they used to insinuate that Hamlet would raise me if they died. They'd say things like, "If something happens to us, don't forget to tell your sister that we love her."

His responses were usually, "Tell her yourself because I'm not getting saddled with her."

It wasn't terribly surprising, considering Hamlet had never considered marriage. All the female werewolves in his year were chosen by other mates, and he was too lazy to battle for the one he liked. He was prompted into taking younger female mates who were left over from their years, but he declined their families' proposals, finding small faults with each female.

I didn't have the benefit of playing with nieces and nephews, or the playful jabs of a sister-in-law when I asked her for help as I slipped clumsily through adolescence. Most of all, though, I felt like my brother despised me.

Sure, we've shared brief hugs over the holidays and jokes about our parents, but he was never close to me. Part of me feels like a piece of my family is missing, and another part is glad he doesn't care about me. It makes it easier to ignore his indifference to his family.

It wasn't uncommon for the older werewolf child to be arrogant and aloof. But even if they were detached, offspring usually clung to one of their parents in times of need. My mother told others that Hamlet ran to her when he was troubled, but truthfully, any challenges he faced were met on his own.

My experiences with Hamlet were one of the reasons I didn't want to have children. I couldn't imagine pouring my heart into raising a cub and having it treat my endearments with loveless necessity.

Unfortunately, I dealt with the same possible future every Sunday when Hamlet graced us with his presence. But it wasn't until a Sunday three months before my Glistening that it weighed on me to the point I broke.

Rymon opened the door and formally welcomed my family. Usually, our parents wouldn't stand on ceremony, but as it was an unofficial rite of passage, they matched his social graces with their own.

I had been required to wear a dress, and it revealed most of my legs, making me feel exposed. My mother had sewn the spring green sundress from one of the patterns she had collected in my childhood. She'd assumed I'd be like her, wearing frilly dresses with practical pockets, but I preferred dark pants, loose tee shirts, and combat boots. The style wasn't uncommon for beings my age, but it was a shock to the culture in which my older parents were raised.

Rymon's parents, Seamus and Gretta, motioned us to a table where Rymon's grandparents were already sitting. We took our seats with them, and I was placed at the end opposite the head of the table, with my father to my right and my brother to my left. Rymon was seated at the head of the table, and as he was the first-born child of young parents, his mother and father flanked him.

Rymon's parents took vows and had him within a year of marriage, so some of his grandparents were still alive. My father's parents had perished in a fire just after I was born, and my mother's father died shortly afterward. My mother told me that my grandmother was one of the casualties during the Overtaking, and her life was extinguished just before Archard finished closing the dome.

From her stories, I knew my mother had been raised by a werewolf who had lost his wife and daughter during the attack, but she never treated his memory differently. Her father had been murdered before she was under the protection of Archard's dome, and she didn't remember him. She recalled her upbringing with her adopted father well, and she honored his memory with reverence.

Rymon had two grandparents, his father's mother and his mother's father, who shared the meal with us. They sat silently and no one attempted to engage them in conversation.

I could hardly eat the bounty of food in front of me. Usually, I could scarf down three turkey legs before the roasted venison made its way around the table, but I was too nervous to do more than pick at the meat in front of me.

No one spoke about the reason for our evening together. Our parents glanced at Rymon and me from time to time and then looked at each other as if they knew a secret about us, and we were too young to understand it. They didn't know that I hadn't voluntarily held hands with Rymon, but they thought they were among two teenagers in love.

Sitting at the table with our families made me both nervous and happy. I was happy to share a meal with people who had known me since I was a cub, but I was nervous about my reaction to Rymon. Eventually, I'd be expected to touch my best friend in the presence of our loved ones, and I was worried that my true feelings would show.

I loved Rymon, and he was my dear friend, but I didn't feel passionate about him. Rymon cared about me beyond a platonic relationship, but so far, I had waved off his advances like troublesome flies.

After dinner, Rymon and I were instructed to go to the bathroom as our families followed us. A metal folding chair was placed in the middle of the room and a white towel was draped over the back.

Rymon sat in the chair and looked at the floor. He was supposed to stare into my eyes as I tied the towel around his neck, but he didn't move his head as I fixed the end of the towel behind his back.

"The first hairs sprouted on his jaw last week," Gretta announced happily. "We were so happy when the ones on his chin grew long enough. I was afraid he wouldn't grow hair until after his Glistening!"

She smiled as she spoke to my mother. My mother grinned back, but her action was forced. Gretta's anxiousness was clear as she chattered about her son's private developments.

"Mom," Rymon groaned. "Please just stop talking."

Rymon's father tried to save him from further embarrassment. "It's perfectly normal, Gretta. Most werewolves get their hair at fifteen, but it's perfectly fine for a cub to peak into adolescence late."

My father's eyebrows rose, and my mother busied herself by buttoning and unbuttoning a button on her dress. We all saw Rymon's humiliation, but we were powerless to stop the comments.

"It doesn't mean he'll be any less of a wolf," Rymon's grandfather piped up. "I was in school with a being who got his hair late, but he went on to father a cub." He paused. "Not right away, though."

Rymon was completely mortified, and my compassion for him grew. I felt the need to help him regain some of his pride.

I steeled my nerves and put his chin in my hand. When he met my eyes, I smiled. "It's my honor to shave you."

The words had been spoken between werewolf mates for generations, and I had heard my mother say them to my father many times. I tried to echo her tone and sincerity, as in my pity, I still felt the same about my friend.

A straight razor had been laid on the counter, and after I lathered his face with his father's shaving cream, I glided it down Rymon's cheeks from his temple to his jaw. Werewolves had to be shaved in a particular way, and I took care with each stroke, referencing the demonstrations my mother had given me on a cantaloupe.

After Rymon's face was clean, I unhooked the towel and handed it to him, allowing him to rub away any stray foam. He grabbed for my hand, and we fumbled fingers until we found a way to comfortably lace them together.

"Thank you for your devotion to me. I look forward to my life with you in it."

It was a beautiful moment, and I could almost see my life with Rymon unfolding, but then my brother spoke. "You missed a spot."

It could have been a joke, and Seamus smiled until he realized that Hamlet was criticizing my work. He reached between us, causing me to straighten and Rymon to pull away. Hamlet brushed just under his chin. "There," he pointed out.

Sure enough, he was right. I had missed a part rarely seen by the public.

Rymon's grandmother gasped. "Legend says, *A spot left behind is a blot on the union.*"

Gretta laughed nervously. "That's not true. There have been many successful marriages that have survived unsuccessful shaves."

"Name one," her mother-in-law challenged.

Gretta put out her index finger, but she couldn't add to it. "Well, I'm sure there's someone."

"Doesn't surprise me," Hamlet said, taking the straight razor and studying the blade. "She's never been able to see anything through."

"Hamlet!" our father snapped at him.

Hamlet stared him down defiantly. "Well, did she finish dance classes or go to the homemaker's classes you paid for?" When my father didn't speak, he went on. "Maybe she could have learned a proper shave if she'd attended just one of those classes. My mother could practically teach the homemaking courses, but does she" —he pointed at me— "ever ask her for any advice?"

I stood with my hand held loosely in Rymon's, and I dropped it. I was tired of everyone's presumptions and my brother's detestable behavior.

"You're one to talk," I barked at Hamlet. "Where's your wife?" I could see the color rising on his plump face until it almost turned purple. "Oh! I know! You weren't good enough for a union."

My mother opened her mouth to stop me, but I spoke over her. "You're just jealous, *Ham*. You never found anyone who wanted to shave you!"

I stormed out of the bathroom, brushing past family members whose faces were a blur. I ran out into the night and away from my obligations.

CHAPTER 7

I didn't stop running until I ran into the dome. It slung me backward, and I ended up on my butt in the grass. My hand went to my forehead, where a knot was already forming, and I screamed into the night, following it with my cries of shame.

Arms wrapped around me, pulling my hands away from my face. I was horrified when I realized Zaffron had responded to my distress.

"Are you okay?" he asked. Concern drew down his eyebrows.

"I'm fine," I choked out, but I couldn't stop sobbing.

"Let me check you out."

He laid me down in the grass, putting one palm tenderly behind my neck. His hands were softer than I expected, and they caressed my injured face.

"You may have a concussion," he observed. "I need to take you to a healer."

"No need," I replied. "I'd be better before we got there."

"Then I will wait with you." He ballooned his cloak out so it didn't tuck under him when he sat next to me.

"Thank you," I told him.

The first few minutes were strained, as neither of us started a conversation. My brain was still rattled from the beating it had taken, and Zaffron wasn't known for easy discussions. Finally, I felt the awkwardness of the situation and sought to fill it with my voice.

"So, what were you doing out tonight?"

"I was shadowing another dragon as he patrolled his perimeter." Zaffron stared up into the sky as we saw it through the dome. "I told him I was taking a break."

"Did he hear me, too?" My humiliation was growing.

"I don't think so," Zaffron said. "I followed you for a while before you hit the barrier."

I looked over at him in disbelief. "You were following me?"

He met my eyes and raised an eyebrow. "You were out after curfew."

I hadn't known it had gotten so late, and when I ran out, I wasn't thinking about the ten o'clock curfew imposed on younger beings. It was enforced loosely, as most of the younger supernaturals were kept at home with two responsible parents, but occasionally, a minor would sneak out to meet friends or a potential mate. Usually, a vampire would find the violators, leaving them at the door of their house after they had bent their necks for a bite.

"I'm sorry," I apologized.

Both of his eyebrows went up. "Why are you telling me? I'm not your parent or your betrothed."

I was still a little raw from my brother's degrading remarks. "I'm not betrothed."

Zaffron laid back on the grass beside me with his hands behind his head, staring at the stars. "Does your little puppy pal know that?"

I had been wrapped up in Zaffron's scent. Not unlike his father, he smelled of soot, but there was an amber quality, almost like the liquid my father drank after a hard day. After hearing him utter the same derogatory name as his father, I sighed heavily, hoping to convey my irritation.

"We are not pups!" I tried to get up, but the world swayed.

Zaffron applied gentle pressure to my arm to move me back onto the grass. He turned his body toward me, and his concern returned. "Are you certain that you don't need a healer? I can fly us to a facility."

"I don't want to go anywhere with you," I bit at him. I felt better when lying down, but I was determined to move as quickly as possible.

"I didn't mean to say that," Zaffron said. "My father says it, and I guess I just picked it up."

It was meant as an apology, and I was expected to acknowledge him. All I could manage was a thin "okay."

The silence stretched again, and I fought against my need to fill it. I picked out a star and concentrated on it.

Suddenly, Zaffron's face hovered over me. "Your eyes are clearer," he remarked. He was only inches from me, and I could smell roasted pork on his breath.

He touched my forehead, rolling his thumb over the spot that had been raised. "You may be healing on your own."

Hadn't he believed me? I was irritated by his insinuation.

"I told you that I could heal myself!"

"It's a noteworthy quality," he said off-handedly. "Do you want to try to get up?"

I grudgingly let him pull me into a sitting position. He stared at me, watching for any signs of distress.

I thought I should say something nice, as he had taken care of me. "Have you ever thought about becoming a healer?"

His jaw clenched, and his lips formed a hard line. "Dragons are not healers."

I rolled my eyes at him. "That sounds like more propaganda from Namon the Impaler."

He turned away quickly, getting to his feet. "I saw you were in trouble, and I helped you. That's hardly a reason to sign up for healing courses."

I decided to lighten the mood. "Well, point them to me if you ever need a reference. I'll be your first satisfied patient."

I was horrified by my words. It had to have been the concussion that caused me to speak that way.

For the first time, Zaffron seemed embarrassed. "I appreciate your offer, but I'm in line for the council."

"Of—Of course," I fumbled.

"I'll fly us to your house now." He stood, and his leather jacket slipped easily down his legs.

"I can walk," I argued, but I almost tripped when I took a step.

"I will be taking you." His words were firm but not unkind.

He approached my side, and I waited for him to pick me up and carry me in flight, much like a bird clutches its meal. He cocked his head as if waiting for me to say something.

"Do I have your permission to carry you home?"

I was shocked by his manners. Dragons lived by a code, and it seemed they wouldn't pick up another person in flight without permission.

I nodded my consent, and he bent to place one arm under my knees and the other behind my back. When he picked me up, he adjusted me too quickly, and my mouth was within inches of his lips. He registered the distance and seemed to consider our closeness.

"Hold onto me."

I did as he requested, and he pushed me up into the sky beneath the dome.

— · —

CHAPTER 8

Allistar didn't show up for school on Monday. After a couple of days, we realized he wasn't coming back.

Fallyn heard he had to go before the council after Breeze and Crisp had reported him, and Rymon told me the unicorn elders watched him to make sure he wouldn't approach the barrier again. Bredek relayed the worst of the news.

"Namon said he couldn't walk under the Glistening Tree."

"Can he do that?"

Bredek's shoulders peaked.

Fiona answered my question. "Probably. Namon sits on the council, and he has a lot of influence over it."

I knew one person who wouldn't be swayed by Namon's opinion, and I walked to his office after my last class of the day.

Lycon was a council member who represented the werewolves. In the structured educational systems humans had in place, he would have been viewed as the principal of our school.

Lycon came up with the idea to name the building where we took classes. He gave the students the power to decide its designation, as they were the ones who would be attending the classes there, and he expected mature responses. He received a rainbow of responses, from comical ideas to simplistic titles. He weeded through the array of suggestions and gave the students three options. After a vote from every student was tallied, Lycon announced the new name of the building was United Pines.

At first glance, it was an odd name for a supernatural school. The building was a school for several races of integrated beings, though, and we were surrounded by the trees common to the Appalachian region. We saw many deciduous trees, like oak and maple caught in eternal summers, but coniferous trees dotted the landscape throughout the year.

The value of the acronym wasn't lost on the students or the teachers. I was used to the posters that read "Move UP in your abilities!" as well as the handwritten notes beneath them that countered with *UP yours.*

Lycon held the most revered position at United Pines, but he had chosen an old broom closet as his office. I knocked on the gray metal door and ran my finger along a couple of the dents before he called me inside.

He had retained the metal shelves and had lined them with books. I tried to read several titles as I squirmed into a seat. Leftover magic caused many of the characters designed by unicorn authors to dance from spine to spine, laughing gleefully as they jumped from one book to the next.

I had borrowed books from Lycon's personal library many times. I'd learned about werewolf forecasts and the history of King Kano's War. I had read a vague prophecy about a dragon who would turn the tide of an oceanic war, and I hoped that being would do it soon. I liked living under the dome's protection, but I yearned to experience life to its fullest, and I couldn't do that while hiding inside a magician's spell.

Lycon had asked a troll to add a small window to his office, and it was open, circulating springtime through the room. A dish of peppermints sat on his desk, and their crisp scent tickled my nose.

I folded my hands in my lap and took in Lycon's aging features. His cloudy brown eyes rested a little too close over his mountain of a nose, little hairs sprouting from its peak and base. He was rumored to be the oldest of our kind, but he had a memory like a steel trap. He knew the names of all the students in the school, and he used them as he passed us in the hallways each day.

"Corryne," he said. "To what do I owe the pleasure of your company?"

"I'm worried about Allistar." I was always direct with him, and he usually respected my forthright manner.

He flipped his silver hair over his shoulder and leaned forward in his seat, steepling his fingers in front of his mouth. He studied me for a moment before he pushed back in his chair. "I won't pretend that your interest in him has gone unnoticed. The only one who appears willfully blind to your attraction is your betrothed."

Red heat wrapped around my neck and face, and I dropped my eyes. "Rymon and I aren't officially—"

He held up his hand. "I'm not passing judgment on you." He rocked back in his ancient leather chair, and it squeaked. "Unicorns are lovely creatures. I fell for a young filly when I was young. Of course, back then, the rules of our kind were different."

I didn't know supernaturals had once been able to intermarry. My surprise must have shown on my face.

Lycon smiled. "That was before King Kano's War and the distrust that followed." His eyes wandered out the window to a time when magical creatures had more choices.

His mental trip to the past was short, and he continued to share his feelings. "The council is made up of eight leaders. Not everyone agrees about the material we press on our youth, but the majority rule."

"But you're respected," I blurted out.

He nodded thoughtfully. "I am. But some challenge my feelings and beliefs for their reasons."

Namon immediately came to my mind. "Have they lived as long as you, though? Do they have your wisdom?"

Lycon's eyebrows shot up. "Dragons and vampires are almost ageless. Who am I to question their sage experiences?"

I dropped my eyes, chastised.

"But you are here about your friend." He swiveled his chair to face me, and I met his gaze. He studied me for a moment as if truly reading my intentions. "Allistar will be fine. He will be present on Glistening Day, but his parents have chosen to finish his lessons at home."

My eyes watered unexpectedly. I hadn't expected the news, but I was surprised I was so upset about it.

"His parents want to keep a closer eye on him," I guessed.

Lycon touched his nose to indicate I was right.

I thanked him for his time, and he dismissed me formally. He called my name before I left.

He stared at me for a moment. He wanted to tell me something but was unwilling to say it. I was beginning to feel self-conscious in the silence when he spoke. "Don't let your future be determined by the past. Sometimes, our best option is the one we have thought about the least."

It wasn't the first time he had given me cryptic advice. Although, I had been much younger when he had spoken veiled words to me. Coincidentally, it was after my first visit to see the talisman.

—·—

CHAPTER 9

I recognized the edges of the dream as it swept me into the past. Part of me knew I was at home in my bed, but I could almost feel the whispering wind of the summer day as I followed my father into the caves.

I had just progressed from my second to third year of classes, and my father was pleased with my progress, so he had taken me to work with him. I was always interested in every aspect of his work, and I wanted to see the talisman. I longed for the day when the responsibilities of his coveted position would fall upon me, and I took in every detail he shared as the caves closed around us.

I hopped beside him, his hand cupping mine until we arrived at the innermost chamber. A red glow emanated from the talisman, beating scarlet echoes against the walls as the fire in the torches flickered. As soon as I entered the area, I could hear marching in my ears. My father continued to talk, oblivious to my growing uncertainties.

Sitali, the vampire on guard, was the first to notice my paling skin and trembling form. As she approached, my father crouched down, said my name, and shook me. I could almost smell his panic. It came to me in waves, reminding me of the scent of the ground after a hard rain.

Sitali must have mentioned pulling me from the room. When I awoke, I was just inside the cave's entrance. My father and the vampire had spoken in whispers, but seeing my eyelids flutter, they cut off their conversation. I had heard their discussion, but I couldn't make sense of it.

At the time, my father shared his position with an aging griffin, Cyprus. Cyprus was unreachable, so my father remained at his post. My mother arrived later, shaking her head with disapproval. In her eyes, I had shamed the family and inconvenienced my father and her. We walked home in silence, her mouth in a thin line and her posture rigid. I looked at my hands and tried to develop new ways of twisting my fingers around.

I stayed in my room for the rest of the day. An official punishment hadn't been issued, but my mother's anger seemed to bubble beneath the surface. I had done nothing wrong, but I humbly kept my head down to atone for any imagined slights.

In the late afternoon, a knock at my bedroom door startled me. My father handed me a peanut butter sandwich in a napkin, and I realized my mother hadn't planned to feed me. Peanut butter was usually a snack.

My father fumbled through some words and told me he thought it would be best if I didn't return to the caves with him. For most of the conversation, he stared at the floor, but then he reached over and hugged me, convinced he had communicated his feelings properly.

Long after he left, I sat with my sandwich in my hand, the napkin vibrating in my vision from my silent sobs. After I dried my tears, I crept to the kitchen. The streetlight cast strange shadows on the antique red and white tiles as I listened for movement in my parents' room. They seemed to be sleeping, and I envied their easy slumber. I finally threw the sandwich—and my hope to follow in my father's footsteps—into the trash.

I lay in bed with the snatches of sentences between my father and Sitali swirling in my head. I couldn't make sense of their words, so I discarded them.

Now, as my dream faded, and my consciousness returned to my comfortable bed, their forgotten words echoed around me as if I was hearing them again.

Do you think she's the one? Sitali spoke.

No, my father affirmed. *She just didn't have enough to eat for breakfast, so she fainted.*

But the ruby pulsated. It reacted to her—

My father cut her off. *She's not the one.*

I woke up in a cold sweat, and I knew several truths at once. First, I'd had a corporeal reaction to the talisman on more than one occasion. Secondly, my father had covered it up and kept me from the necklace until the field trip. And most alarming of all, I suspected that there was a prophecy about me.

—·—

CHAPTER 10

An eight-year-old that belonged to any race of beings shouldn't wander off alone, but since our communities were governed by the iron hand of the council, offspring who gathered in groups could go from one destination to another with little fear.

When I was young, I didn't have a group of friends, so I went everywhere with Rymon. I dragged him to the outskirts of a forbidden forest where vampires went to feed, and I took him on adventures where we swam in an eerie lake and explored a property with a driveway and no house.

We rode our bicycles to Lycon's house and deposited them in his front yard. Little garden gnomes peeked up from the landscaping, beckoning us onto the porch. I was glad gnomes hadn't been threatened during King Kano's War. Their faux jovial faces seemed worse than their cousins', the leprechauns, who gave me the creeps. All underground creatures were unhappy and devious by nature, or I thought they were. I had read about them in one of Lycon's books before it gave me nightmares, and I'd had to return it.

Rymon bounced in front of me and rang the doorbell. A recorded message in Lycon's voice played over an unseen speaker: *"Hello. If you are selling something, I do not open my door to solicitors. If you are a vampire, please check under the gnome with the red hat for a surprise. If you are a friend, however, enter and be welcome!"*

"I wonder what's under the red hat?" Rymon commented, turning to look at me with his eyebrows raised.

I shrugged. Given the age-old tensions between werewolves and vampires, I doubted it was anything good.

"Should we just go in?" he asked as he opened the door.

I followed him inside, and the scents of the forest floor hit me. Werewolves lived in a neighborhood with brick houses of similar construction so—other than the foyer—the house seemed to have been built by the same blueprint as the other structures.

I found the living room in the same place as the one in my home, and I noted the bookcases along the walls. The only space was above the fireplace, where a picture of a young girl peering around a stone wall looked upon a castle in the sky. It was unsurprising, as Lycon believed strongly in the power of magic.

The opinion on magic had changed since the dome had encased the beings beneath it. Rationally, everyone should have understood that they were protected by something beyond their scope of understanding, but some beings—primarily werewolves—did not accept the dome's mystical origins.

Lycon stepped into the room, leaning over the book in his hand. "To what do I owe the pleasure?" He didn't look up from the pages, but I believed his attention was equally divided between the book and us.

"My girlfriend wants to know about the talisman," Rymon spoke for me. He knew it upset me when he called me his girlfriend, but he was too unruly to control his energy and thoughts at the same time.

"I'm not your girlfriend," I hissed at him. "And I can talk for myself."

Lycon looked up from his book and closed it with a snap. "Rymon, why don't you go into that room" —he pointed to an area to our left— "and look at the train set."

Rymon's eyes lit up. The town under the dome had once been bustling with railroad activity. Now, the track was cut off as it entered and exited our town. The track continued inside the town, though, one engine remained that pulled a solitary group of passengers in an old car. It only ran during special events, but Rymon was always the first one in line to ride it.

My friend rushed into the room, leaving me alone with Lycon. He sat in a blue armchair and invited me to do the same on the adjacent loveseat.

"What would you like to know about the necklace?"

I fidgeted, twirling my thumbs over each other. "I-I guess I want to know everything about it."

He chuckled. "We'd be here for a week if I told you everything I knew and what was speculated about the talisman."

I looked up at him. I'd already decided I wasn't going to tell him what happened to me in the cave, but I wanted to know something, and my parents withheld any information about it—other than my father's welcome speech to the weekly visitors.

"I'll give you a concise explanation," he decided.

I waited as Lycon pulled a book out from under his chair. He'd read it recently, as it wasn't dusty. Many of the pages were dog-eared, and when he opened it, sections were marked with a rainbow of highlights.

"Several decades ago, King Kano waged a war against every being who refused to follow him. A mass genocide resulted, driving our kind to the greatest magician of the age, Archard."

"Did you meet him?" I interjected. I'd always been fascinated by Archard when I saw the pictures of him in the books. His eyes seemed to look into me, and they simultaneously excited and frightened me.

"I did," Lycon confirmed. "And he was as amazing in person as in the text you've read about him."

He glanced inside his book and turned to a section highlighted in purple. He read, "Amalthea brought Archard the necklace and laid it at his feet. Even though our wise and valiant magician was nearly spent, he took strength from the charm and sealed the terrible King Kano and his watery minions in the darkest depths of the ocean."

Even at a tender age, I knew that mermaids were evil. The beings under the dome were stuck here because of them.

"Do you see anything wrong with the passage I read?" he asked, pausing before he turned a page. "Any similarities or duplicities?"

I struggled to find something wrong with the words I'd heard. In the end, I could only shake my head.

"I see." I could tell he was disappointed, so I tried again.

"Maybe Archard made all of us prisoners," I guessed.

Something sparked in Lycon's eyes. "Go on."

Making the observation had been hard enough, and I worried I'd let him down when I tried to dissect my statement. "He probably shouldn't have forced them to stay in the water when we were already in the dome."

He seemed to weigh my words, looking up at the ceiling before he addressed me. "But would Kano have waged more destruction without anyone to oppose him?"

"I don't know," I replied honestly. "Maybe Archard just wanted to lessen the chance that Kano would find the dome and breach it."

He pointed at me. "That's a good point, but the elves are expert hunters and trackers, and they laid marks where the dome had risen. They didn't let the sun go down before they placed stakes around the perimeter."

I sighed. I had given up trying to rationalize a magician's actions.

Lycon sensed my frustration and moved on. "Not much is known about the spell he cast or all the implications of it, but the plan he made for us came at a high price. Archard lost his life, and his sister is presumed dead."

I was quiet. It was the only suitable response until he spoke again.

"The book was written by Cyprus. I think you know him."

"He works with my father."

Lycon nodded, as he had expected my answer. "He was with us when Archard revealed the blueprints of the dome."

I felt like I was in the room with a living piece of history. Between Cyprus's book and Lycon, I had mountains of first-hand information within my reach. The dome was my home, and I knew no other place, so its creation was as interesting as the origins of the universe.

A train whistle tooted, and Rymon's laughter carried to us. Sounds of a train chugging down an artificial track followed.

"I think your friend has been entertained," Lycon chuckled.

I smiled thinly. Lycon seemed to read my expression.

"Is there something more specific you'd like to ask me?"

"May I borrow that book?" I asked him, nodding at the tome in his lap.

His grip around it tightened. "I'm afraid this text is a constant study. I can't part with it."

I went back to fidgeting, surprised by his answer. Usually, Lycon granted all my requests, but he seemed especially attached to Cyprus's book. I berated myself for asking if Lycon would lend me his most treasured book.

Lycon jumped up. Still spritely for his age, he moved nimbly across the floor and raised onto the tips of his toes to edge a book out of the side of one of his tall shelves.

"You can borrow this one, though," he said, looking inside the cover and shaking his head. "On second thought, my dear Corryne, keep it. You'll give it a good home."

I ran my hand over the leathery cover when he handed it to me. There was no author or title, but the cover reflected the maroon tones of the ruby in the talisman.

"Thank you," I breathed, stroking the spine like he'd handed me a living being. "It's beautiful."

Rymon ran into the room, red-faced and breathing heavily. "He has H and O cars!"

I had no idea what that meant, but I was certain my friend would fill me in on our walk home. I thanked Lycon for his hospitality and rushed after Rymon, who had bounced down the steps and twisted his ankle. He cried out and recovered quickly, healing faster than most beings of our kind.

Later that night, I sat with the book Lycon had given me. It was full of information, and I decided to separate it into sections, concentrating on one area of the book at a time. The first part discussed mermaids, and I thought it was the perfect place to begin. Much to my surprise, though, it wasn't a documentary about King Kano. Instead, it outlined a mermaid's defenses and special abilities. A picture of a teenager with red hair and blue-green eyes had been drawn. She seemed familiar, even though there were no mermaids under the dome.

After reading the chapter about mermaids, my opinion about them wavered. At first, it started as a notion that they weren't completely bad, and it morphed into pity.

I finally understood the point Lycon had tried to make. The mermaids were contained in much the same way as the beings under the dome, but they weren't there by choice. It made me wonder how many truly believed in King Kano's cause, and how many were only looking for a way out.

CHAPTER 11

My dream and the subsequent reflections gave me the drive to do something about my feelings. Even though I started walking in that direction, I was surprised when my feet led me to Allistar's house. I moved up the steps confidently, but I lost my resolve when footsteps approached the door and it opened.

Allistar stood in the doorway. At first, his eyebrows rose in curiosity, but then his expression changed, dropping into an angry stare. "What do you want?"

I faltered. "I— I wanted to see if you were okay."

He took a step back and held his arms wide, indicating he was fine. "Now you can go."

He started to shut the door in my face, but I stopped him. I used too much force, and the door cracked under the pressure. Allistar pursed his lips, looking from me to the damaged door.

"I'll pay to have it fixed." The crack was hardly noticeable, but it was my temper that had caused the blemish.

"Look, haven't you done enough?" He threw up his hands and shouted at me. "I can't go back to school, Felicity won't speak to me, and I don't know if they're going to let me walk around the tree on Glistening Day!"

I focused on the part of his distress that affected me the most. "Felicity broke up with you?" I heard how selfish I sounded, but I didn't care.

Allistar stomped toward me, his nostrils flaring. He was so close that his temper rained down on me in hot, uneven breaths.

Even though he was angry, I could feel it had more to do with him than with me. I wouldn't have been afraid of him anyway, but I calmly stared back at him, willing him to make the next move.

I don't know how long we stood there with Allistar's anger raging, but I was acutely aware of every rattling car or neighbor who passed us. I felt like we were suspended in our own bubble of time, surrounded by every emotion.

I stared into his purple eyes, seeing wisps of clouds seeming to roll through them. I wondered if he stared into my plain brown eyes and saw the spark of my passion for him hiding there.

I imagined his rage cooling into indifference or flaming into something more. In that case, I preferred his anger, and I longed for him to grab me and press his lips to mine.

Allistar turned on his heel and stomped into his house, slamming the door. He didn't move away from it, but after a few minutes, I left, my smile expanding across my face.

As I went through my nightly routine, I started to doubt myself. *What had I been thinking? Why would I show up at Allistar's house and act happy that his betrothed had dumped him?*

I couldn't sleep. I tossed and turned until I heard a sharp sound outside my window. I was startled, but when I heard it again, I dropped into a crouch, ready to attack any creature dumb enough to tap on a werewolf's window.

"Corryne?" The voice was whispered but distinct.

I advanced cautiously, peeking through the eyelets in the blinds. I could smell him before I saw him, his strawberry scent drifting to me through two panes of glass.

I pushed my window open carefully. My parent's bedroom was on the other side of the hall, but their hearing was as good as mine.

"What are you doing here?"

Allistar looked down at his feet. "I don't—" His eyes shot up and met mine. "My dad says that humans have an adage that they use when two people don't belong together."

"Is it about the bird and the fish falling in love?"

"Yeah."

I took his chin in my hand, keeping his eyes locked on mine. "The fish didn't have a way to turn into a bird, though."

It hit him, and the starbursts in his irises seemed to expand and contract as he stared at me. "You'd do that for me?"

"Yes," I whispered, realizing I meant it.

He climbed through my window, his long limbs making it easy to step through. I moved out of the way, crossing my arms to protect myself from the chilly night. Allistar noticed my discomfort and eased the window back into place. "It's colder at night now," he said nervously.

We stood awkwardly in my room. We were too shy to embrace our budding romance. My gaze never left his face, even though he glanced away several times. Finally, I rolled my eyes and stepped up to him. I reached up and laced my fingers behind his neck, and his arms circled my waist.

He leaned down, and the warmth of his lips on mine melted any doubt I ever had about us. Allistar seemed more resolved as his tongue searched my mouth, and he led me to my bed. We kissed for what seemed like minutes but may have been hours, and when my alarm woke me up for school, we both shot up off the bed.

Allistar had remained fully dressed, so he climbed through my window while I rushed around my room. We didn't kiss before he left, and I wondered if we were together or if he had changed his mind.

I sat down with my mother and father at the breakfast table, and I hardly returned their attempts at conversation. My father was busy looking through the computer advertisements for job openings.

"There's nothing," he announced in defeat.

Usually, creatures under the dome would inherit jobs from their parents—unless someone died who didn't have an heir. Hamlet had been expected to become the curator of the necklace, but after years of assumptions, he'd left our parents' home for a policeman's position. When I was young, I had been groomed to care for the talisman until the day my father took me to work with him.

My mother reached across the table. "It's okay, Kurt. You'll find something."

He covered her hand with his own, grateful for her support.

My father sniffed the air. "What's that smell?" His nose pointed upward, searching for the source of the scent.

I didn't want his senses to lead him to my bedroom, so I searched my mind for a reasonable explanation. "I let Felicity borrow my hoddie during the class trip."

My parents stared at me in disbelief. I was allowed to have other supernatural friends, but it was an unspoken rule that they were to be kept separate.

"Was she in your group?" my father asked.

"No," I answered carefully. "She was in Aella's group, but she was cold on the bus, so I let her borrow it."

My mother stared at my hoddie with her lip curled up. "Why didn't you give it to me to launder? How can you stand wearing it with her smell all over it?"

My father was more accepting of other species, but he tempered his beliefs when he was around his wife. He often spoke about the equality within our boundaries and the discrimination his ancestors had experienced before Archard's dome was in place. Often called "dogs," other beings considered werewolves the lowliest of magical creatures. Other beings tormented us, especially unicorns, who frowned on our shifting canine forms and our inability to control our tempers.

My grandfather was to blame for my mother's spiteful feelings against other races of supernaturals, and he remembered the slights he suffered as he mopped the floors of a high-rise building and guarded it against attacks. He was a skilled guard, and the building was spotless, but the unicorns and fayries who conducted their business in the building, treated him with contempt. He grew to hate them, and he almost defected when the Druids approached him about the location of the rest of the magical creatures. My grandmother stopped him, but whatever she said to him didn't quench the fires of hate in his heart against unicorns and fairies, and he passed that hate on to my mother.

I shrugged my shoulders. "I didn't really think about it."

"Let me wash it now." She held her hand out for my hoodie.

"I'll be late for school, and it's colder this morning."

My mother and father exchanged a look, the unicorn smell temporarily forgotten. "It's already started," she said to him.

My father's mouth formed a grim line. "It started the day I was dismissed."

"What's really going on?" I interjected.

My father rubbed one of his eyes. "It's nothing to worry about right now."

"When am I supposed to worry about it? Should I ask you again when the sky starts falling?"

"That would be a better time to run than to ask questions." My mother spoke her words without humor.

I rolled my eyes and stood up. "I'm going to school. Maybe someone there will tell me what's going on."

I walked next door and knocked, but Rymon's mother told me he had already left for school. I was confused, but I waved at her and hurried down the porch steps. My friend had walked to school with me every day since our first day of classes.

I saw Rymon in our first class. He had a black hoodie pulled over his head, and I couldn't see his face. Fiona had been talking to the back of his head, but when she noticed me, she pretended to look for something in her bag.

I sat down in my usual seat, turning around to talk to him. I could see his profile, and his nose was red.

"What's wrong?" I asked.

When he sneered at me, his red-rimmed eyes and the puffiness beneath them shocked me. I almost recoiled from the venom in his words.

"Who visited you last night, Corryne?"

Heads turned, and I worried about my secret. I wasn't ready to tell people I planned to shift into a unicorn on Glistening Day. Besides, it was all so new. I wasn't certain if Allistar second-guessed our rash kisses last night. After all, he hadn't kissed me before he left.

My silence spurred rumors, and by lunch, my friends weren't really speaking to me. Fiona and Bredek tried to stay neutral, but they believed Rymon had the moral high ground.

I may never have formally accepted him as my beaux, but everyone, including Rymon, believed we would take vows after our Glistenings. I should have had the decency to tell him about my relationship with Allistar instead of letting him find out. To my credit, though, I hadn't known I was in a relationship until I pulled Allistar into my room.

How had Rymon found out we were together? Had Allistar called him? It seemed unlikely, but guys could be territorial. I dismissed the notion as soon as I thought it. Allistar wasn't a jealous being.

I took my tray to the recycler, hoping to leave the lunchroom and spend a few quiet minutes in my next class before it filled up. Felicity caught my eye and strode up to me. "I hope you like what's left after he's been with the human." She flipped her hair and smiled. Two fairies flanked her with their lips pursed and their arms crossed. "He's still watching her, you know."

I rolled my eyes, but I wondered about Felicity's words for the rest of the school day. *Was there another place along the barrier where he could see the human? Was I his only stop last night, or had he been to the edge of the dome before he visited me?*

Just before the last bell rang, Rymon purposely bumped into me. Papers flew off the top of my book, but I didn't make a move to pick them up. At first, I thought he was only going to stare at me, but then he narrowed his eyes. "I hope he's worth it."

He walked away from me, and the friendship I thought would never end.

— · —

CHAPTER 12

I convinced myself that I had ruined my friendships over a few stolen kisses in the night, and after a brief lapse of reason the previous night, Allistar had decided he didn't return my feelings. When the smell of strawberries filled my senses, I was glad to see Allistar fall into step beside me.

"You're hard to catch," he commented.

He took my arm and led me in the direction of the unicorn community. The houses there were well-maintained by werewolves, and two of my brethren were tending a yard just before the welcome sign. I took my arm away from Allistar, but he pulled it back.

"You're going to have to get used to this," he scolded.

"I thought we'd wait to tell everyone after I shifted on Glistening Day."

I caught the smile on his profile. "You'll still be Corryne. Everyone is still going to stare. You might as well give them something to talk about now." He chuckled and laid his head on mine for a moment. The shadow we cast on the ground looked like a lumpy rainbow.

We crossed the barrier into the unicorn's section, and he broke away from me. He walked backward, extending his arms in a grand gesture. "Welcome to my *neigh*borhood." He grinned proudly at his joke.

"Hardy-har-har." I shook my head. "Horse jokes."

He rejoined me and put his thin arm over my shoulders. We walked to his house, and he led me through the door as if it were the most natural thing in the world.

Allistar left me in the living room, but he returned quickly with snacks and drinks. I had stood awkwardly where he'd left me, but when he reappeared, I joined him and sat on the couch.

The room was decorated colorfully, with teal furniture and shell-pink curtains. I almost expected the smell of cotton candy to hit my nose, but Allistar's strawberry scent filled the room.

I wasn't comfortable eating the popcorn he put on the table, but I grabbed the water. It had been a long walk from school, and my nervousness made my mouth dry.

Allistar laid back on the couch and put his arms behind his head. "So, when did you start liking me?"

I spit out my water. My choking fit wasn't attractive, but Allistar patted my back and brought a towel to soak up the mess. Once I was okay and the mess was cleaned, he asked his question again.

Even though I could feel the heat rising from my chest and blanketing my face with red warmth, I dug for an honest answer. I thought back to the moment I knew I had a crush on him. "We hadn't been in class long. I heard you sing."

Allistar nodded twice. "I have a good voice."

I agreed, but I thought about the other members of his species. All unicorns could sing like the robins that flittered just beyond the dome. In fact, Felicity lifted her voice on a beautiful falsetto key every time she was given a page of lyrics.

He bounced forward from the back of the couch, bringing his face inches from mine. He ran his eyes across my face, studying me. "I wonder what you'll look like when you're a unicorn."

I had thought of it briefly. "How do you think I'll change?" I offered him a smile, hoping for a compliment.

He leaned back a little and squinted, considering my question. "You'll have a softer voice." We both chuckled at that. "Your arms and legs will be a little longer, and your eyes will turn blue or purple. That'll look good with the silver streak in your hair unless it all turns blonde, white, or silver." He put his hands around my arms, bringing me into his lap. "You'll look really good next to me."

Allistar planted a soft kiss on my lips. He leaned me back onto the couch.

"Where are your parents?" I asked, nervously glancing around.

"They work as healers. They'll be gone until after dark."

I allowed him to trace the line on my jaw. He was slow and kind. He delivered each kiss expertly, and I felt it from my lips to my toes.

At first, he kept pressing himself against me, and I invented new ways of maneuvering my body to keep our make-out session as innocent as possible. Once, he broke away and remarked, "We'll exchange our vows in a couple of months. Let me be close to you."

I shook my head and pushed him off me. "We just started" —I motioned between us— "this last night. I'm not ready to jump into anything."

He raised a perfectly penciled eyebrow. "But you expect me to believe you're going to change your biology for me?"

He had a point, but I was really irritated with him for making it. "Look, I need to go home."

Allistar slid the back of his fingers across my cheek, and his tender touch stopped me. "You don't want to leave," he whispered. "You want to stay. Because if you leave, all you'll do is think of me." He touched his top lip to my bottom lip. "Why not enjoy the time we have together?"

My resolve puddled on the floor at his feet while he kissed me. My mind and body were lost in his lips and swirling tongue, but when his hands started to explore me again, I stopped him. "I need to go. This is too much too fast."

He let out a long, heavy sigh and pointed to the door. "Make your choice."

I instantly steeled. *Was he giving me an ultimatum?*

It was easy for me to leave, but as I walked home, I wondered if Allistar and I were still together. If this was the way our relationship ended, who would share vows with me after my Glistening? My relationship with Rymon was ruined, and I'd be lucky if he ever thought of me as a friend again.

I almost made it back to the werewolf community when I heard swift feet behind me. Allistar stopped in front of me, not even winded. "Hey, shouldn't I walk you home or something?"

"I don't need you to do me any favors," I shot back, not even looking at him.

"Where's that coming from?"

I stopped and put my hands on my hips. "You told me to make my choice. Well, I did, and I chose me."

He put both hands in front of him. "Whoa! I just meant for you to choose whether you wanted to stay or go home."

I stared up at him skeptically, drawing my eyebrows together.

"I would have walked you home, but I couldn't move." He looked down at his pants.

I set my jaw and tossed my eyes up at the sky. I took off, walking faster than I had when he'd approached me.

"Hey!" he called after me. "What did I do wrong?"

I turned on my heel, jabbed my finger into his chest, and shouted at him. "You may have been able to do things like that with Felicity, but we've only been together for about a day! I'm not that easy."

I stormed off, inwardly groaning when I saw two of my kind filter out onto their porches. They had heard the scene I had caused in the street.

Allistar seemed undeterred by my outburst or the onlookers. He sauntered up beside me with renewed confidence. "So, we are together."

He searched for my eyes, but I willfully stared ahead. Finally, I stopped and crossed my arms over myself. We were within sight of my house, but I didn't want my parents to see me with him.

"Yeah."

Allistar lifted my chin and brought his face to mine. "You're going to be a beautiful unicorn," he insisted. His breath on my skin caused me to involuntarily shiver. He seemed satisfied by the effect he was having on me.

He sensed my reluctance to announce our relationship to the beings in my community, and I was afraid he'd take advantage of the moment to make me show them I had feelings for a unicorn. His ego was strong, so I was relieved when he left without kissing me.

—·—

CHAPTER 13

In truth, Rymon had given me my first kiss, and now that he was mad at me, it constantly plagued my thoughts.

It had been my idea to lie to our parents about going to the park. We were thirteen, and we didn't play on the swings and slides, but it had been a popular hangout for teens in the afternoon and evening. My mother and father were oblivious to any other intentions as Rymon bounced by the door, his black shirt accentuating the tone of his developing muscles.

I hadn't told Rymon that I wanted to go to the outskirts of our territory, and he had blanched when I lifted the loose wooden planks on the fence that bordered it. He was so pale that I could almost see through him.

"T-That's the v-vampire's zone," he stuttered.

I lifted the boards higher, motioning for him to go through. "They don't hunt there all the time. It's not even close to their neighborhood."

The vampires lived on the other side of the dome. The zone appropriated for their feeding frenzies bordered several other supernatural communities, and I was convinced that they wouldn't drift close to my area, hoping that they satiated their hunger just beyond their border.

When Rymon didn't move, I went through the fence, crossing into a forest with deep underbrush. By the time I reached a worn path, Rymon was behind me, gripping the back of my shirt in his hand. I tried to pry his fingers off my clothes, but he wouldn't let go.

The sounds of the forest came alive around us. We were quiet, but our feet betrayed us by snapping twigs and vibrating the ground.

Werewolves weren't reared to step lightly, as we could overtake our prey within seconds of spotting them, so our experience with moving stealthily was limited.

"What if one of our kind is here?" Rymon whispered. A bird called down at us.

I let out a sigh. "Then we'd be eaten." His grip on me tightened, and I thought of something to help alleviate some of his anxiety. "The full moon doesn't happen for another two weeks."

His fingers loosened and let go. "I'm acting like a scared cub." His statement was meant more for himself than for me, so I didn't respond.

The woods cleared and opened upon a beach with firmly packed sand. Soft waves of water gently licked the shore as if something large had been dropped into the lake and made ripples on its otherwise glassy surface.

I felt drawn to the water. As a werewolf, I'd never cared for it one way or the other, but I needed to touch the lake, and I did. Rymon pulled on my other arm, urging me back.

"Let's go, Corryne," he whispered, looking from left to right.

The lake was serene, and I'd never seen anything more lovely than its gray-blue water. "Don't touch me!" I shouted at him, jerking my arm away. I rose and stared out at the lake, and it seemed to go on forever. "Why are you acting like such a baby?"

Any other time, Rymon would have argued with me, asserting his dominance, but his eyes darted and his hand trembled when he pointed to the forest. "Don't you hear it?"

"Hear what?" I couldn't detect any sounds from the trees.

"That's just it!" he hissed. "The birds and squirrels were going crazy until you stepped out of the woods." He lowered his voice. "Now everything's quiet."

I had to admit he was right, but I didn't care. All I wanted was to put my feet in the lake. Midway through taking off my shoes, I decided I wanted Rymon to go with me, and after he repeatedly denied my attempts to pull him in with me, I did the only thing I thought would draw him into the water.

He turned his head away as soon as my shirt came off. "What are you doing?"

I was glad he respected me, but I needed him to swim in the lake with me. I couldn't describe my desire to lure him, except that the feeling was almost as strong as my need to submerge myself in the lake. "I don't have a bathing suit, and I'm going for a swim." I touched his hand, dancing my fingers over his palm. "Go with me."

He shook his head, deliberately averting his eyes. "You're not acting like yourself. I think a vampire is trying to get you into the water."

Vampires could hypnotize humans, drawing them in and then erasing their memories. It was harder for them to control the thoughts of other magical creatures, but werewolves were the easiest beings to compel, making the tensions rawer between the races. Genetically speaking, vampires lived long lives, and werewolves burned out quickly, so vampires toyed with them, never caring about the short-lived repercussions.

I shrugged, unmoved by my friend's warning. I dove into the water, and I hardly felt its chill.

The lake was clearer beneath the surface, and I could almost see to the bottom. Two broken rowboats jutted up like jagged teeth, and an open umbrella drifted across the sand as if it were carried by the wind.

Something tugged at my foot.

I tried to pull away, but it held tightly, preventing me from turning around to label it. It dragged me deeper, and I cried out, only letting out bubbles of my reserved air. My fear heightened and cleared my mind. *Why was I in the water? Had it really been my decision to dive under the surface?*

I'd never swum underwater, so I doubted my control over my mind. Whatever had me was supernatural, and it had pulled me to the depths of its home.

Rymon stood over me, dripping large drops of water onto my face. "Corryne!" he shouted into my face, even though he was only inches away.

I tried to answer, but I only succeeded in releasing a gush of water from my mouth. I felt simultaneously better and worse, as I could breathe but a coughing fit raked across my throat.

"I thought you were dead," Rymon repeated as he sat on the shore and buried his face in his hands.

"Something had me," I told him. "How did you get me away?"

"I just grabbed you," he replied, shaking his head in his hands. When he looked up, his expression was pained, as if he were barely holding back his tears. "You were floating in the water, and when I got you up here, you didn't move."

I took him in my arms, and he released his emotions.

Werewolves aren't supposed to cry. No one tells us that, but it's ingrained in every action and reaction. I let my friend's tears hit my shoulders, and I didn't discuss it with anyone, even him.

"Thank you for pulling me out of the water."

He wiped his eyes, but tears still glistened on his lashes. "I was so glad I took that CPR—"

"Whoa!" I held up my hand. "Do you mean you put your mouth on me?"

He dared to appear smug. "Yeah. I kind of had to, or you would have died."

"It's just that—" I tried to find the right way to say it. "That was my first kiss."

He laughed, but when a startled bird flew out of a nearby bush, he quietened and spoke in whispers. "That wasn't a kiss."

"Your lips were on my lips," I insisted. "You kissed me."

"It was the kiss of life," he shot back, amused at my distress. "Would you have rather whatever had you in the water put its lips on you?"

I shook my head, but unexpected tears threatened. Rymon scooted close to me and wrapped his arms around my shoulders. I didn't cry, though.

"I thought it would be more special," I went on, throwing one of my hands up. "At least, I'd imagined I'd be conscious of it."

"You've thought about your first kiss?" Rymon's voice had taken on a husky tone.

I nodded, not seeing the change in him. I looked out onto the water, feeling as if I'd been robbed of a choice, even though Rymon had done the right thing.

He stood up and walked to the edge of the water. I worried that he had been somehow urged to dive into it, but just before I issued a warning, he picked up my discarded shirt and brought it to me, letting it fall within reach. He didn't look at me, and as I thought back to our conversation, I remembered that his eyes were always on my face. I didn't know what he saw when he dragged me out of the water, but I doubted his panicked mind registered anything sensual about the experience.

I slipped my dry shirt over my head, thankful for its warmth. I started to shiver, and I hugged my arms around my chest. Rymon sat down behind me, wrapping me in his arms. He focused his energy, and I was warmer within minutes. I looked back at him to thank him, but he seemed to tremble with undiscovered passion.

It was a shock to me, as I had only felt the warmth of his embrace, so I jumped up. He scrubbed his face and asked me if I wanted to stare at the water for a few minutes. Misreading his need to stay a few minutes longer, I threw my hands up and stalked into the forest. My brash action was all he needed to drive him back into the woods, and within seconds, he was by my side, walking awkwardly.

"How am I going to explain my wet clothes and hair?" I voiced.

Rymon was quick with a lie. "I'll tell your parents that some little kids soaked us at the park." He studied my dry shirt. "We may have to stop at a hose or a fountain on the way there, though."

Once we had figured out a way to explain our appearances, my mind wandered back to the kiss I didn't get to share with the person I loved. I had imagined it would be magical, but it was only a necessity.

By the time the fence was in sight, I had rationalized that someone I loved had kissed me. It may not have been romantic, but my first kiss hadn't been taken from me or stolen away by someone who made promises with no intention of fulfilling them.

At the fence, Rymon grabbed my hand, turning me to him. "Corryne, I still don't think I took your first kiss, but since you feel that way, may I kiss you?"

He trailed his fingers down my cheek and brushed my lips with his fingers. I didn't tingle with anticipation, but I let him lean in.

Rymon may not have technically kissed me, but the act was the same in my young mind. I looked at a subsequent kiss as a fulfillment of the feeling on my side. He was allowing me to make a choice. I could refuse to kiss him, and we wouldn't talk about it, leaving the experience in the same place as a lot of purposely avoided moments in our friendship, or I could choose to give him my first kiss.

In seconds, I knew it was the right choice for me. Even if I found another mate, I felt I would never be as secure as I was at that moment with Rymon.

"I won't do it unless you tell me it's okay," he said.

I nodded.

No sooner had I given my consent than his mouth connected with mine. His lips parted, and I took the cue to allow his entry. He snaked his tongue into my mouth and pushed against mine. I wasn't certain about the proper way to kiss, as I hadn't read about it, and I had an older brother instead of an older sister, so I went along with the motion. Something felt strange about the way our mouths moved together, and even though I'd told Rymon that he could kiss me, I almost felt like I was still blocking him with my tongue.

When I pulled away, he stared at me with lidded eyes, and I knew he hadn't felt my reluctance to give myself over to him. He leaned back into me with his mouth open, and I took a step back, grabbing one of his hands.

"Thank you for making me feel better," I said.

He smiled, trying to tug me back to him. "I'd do it again if you'd let me."

"I'll think about it." I tried to smile, but I could tell by his face that I wasn't convincing.

"What's wrong?" He let go of my hand and put his fingers to his mouth as if the touch of his lips had offended me. "Did I do it wrong?"

"No." I shook my head and laughed. "Besides, I wouldn't know the difference anyway."

"Me either," he confided. "I was saving that for my betrothed."

I don't know what I would have said. I was too flustered by his comment to do more than feel my face flush and my mouth open for words my brain couldn't find.

By some divine intervention, I was saved. A loud noise erupted behind us, and Rymon and I bolted through the fence before it reached us. Once we were safe on the other side, we stood motionless until something hit the boards, causing us both to jump. I thought I heard Rymon cry out, but we never talked about it.

I thought about my good times with Rymon more often since he was mad at me. Before, he had usually been with me, only at his house for some meals and to sleep. I imagine it had hurt him deeply to see Allistar climb through my window when Rymon thought he was my first and only kiss.

Rymon seemed to be the first casualty on the battlefield of my heart, and if I was honest with myself, I knew he didn't deserve it. I should have been clearer about my feelings, but I had been afraid I'd lose his friendship. It had happened anyway, though, and just like those stolen moments, our friendship seemed to be forgotten.

— · —

CHAPTER 14

The next few weeks at school were hard. Rymon wouldn't look in my direction, and my fayrie friends hardly acknowledged me. Bredek interacted with me, but he was only polite. I pretended to be shocked when he told me that Rymon had seen Allistar sneak into my bedroom window after he'd heard our whispered voices. Rymon's bedroom window lined up with mine, so it wasn't a surprise.

I spent my afternoons with Allistar. We didn't go to his house often, so we weren't tempted to take our relationship further than it should go. Most of the time, I met him at the border where Rymon and I found him on the day of the field trip. He people-watched, but I never saw the beautiful human, so I kept my jealousy reigned.

The dome seemed to be disappearing from the top. Each day a little more melted away, taking our protection from King Kano with it. The council members scheduled meetings, and defenses were prepared, but I never really felt involved in the preparations, so it was easy to stay swept away in my budding romance with Allistar.

The rays of the moon didn't fall on me directly, but there were times when I could almost hear it sing to me. The sound was high-pitched and awakened a primal urge that left me yearning for blood. I satisfied the craving with the meat in the refrigerator, understanding the reason werewolves were driven mad by the force of the moon.

One morning, I was sitting in class, exchanging strained pleasantries with Fallyn, when two armed vampires marched into our classroom. The teacher wasn't in sight, and they delivered a speech about loyalty to our kinds and the fight upon us.

"Can't we just stay here?" Felicity asked them. "King Kano may not realize anything has happened to the dome."

The first vampire, who had a dark beard fashioned to a point, answered her. "As the dome disappears, so does the town's invisibility. We think King Kano's spies have already noticed a difference."

The other vampire lifted his muscular arm to stop the murmurs in our class and added, "There are also some sympathizers to the crowned King of the Sea within our borders. We're afraid they have already found a way to send him messages."

"Blood traitors!" Rymon barked. I nodded my head until he poked my back. "You're no different, Corryne. You and your stupid unicorn boyfriend are one of the reasons the dome is weakening."

"Corryne, Maureen's daughter?" The first vampire spoke to me while the other one glared cruelly. "I never would have expected Maureen's yelp to find a unicorn mate." He motioned to my friends around me—mostly fayries. "But then again, what could she expect from you with such spritely company."

A vicious smile inched across his face, and I felt the stares of the other students on me. I stood up and walked out of the class as two werewolf boys jeered. I knew them, but we didn't hang out, so their rude gestures were quickly dismissed.

Rudi, a female of my kind, glanced over at Rymon. She was betrothed to Mingan, another male in our year, but his tech-savvy expressions and introverted mannerisms were opposite to her outgoing, egocentric ways. She'd eyed Rymon a few times, and even though I didn't have romantic feelings for him, I doubted that Rudi and Rymon would make a good match.

Out of all the beings in my classroom, Rymon's words stung me the most. I was certain to keep my face blank and my head held high as I left the room.

I thought about going to Lycon's office, but I couldn't face his disappointment. *What if he was against my relationship with Allistar, too?* He may have had a crush on a unicorn once, but he hadn't mentioned acting on it. I found a door that led to the part of the school that hadn't been reconstructed, and I bolted into the first unlocked room.

It smelled like fresh lemon cleanser, even though the area was outdated and fitted for other uses. A blood pressure cuff hung on the wall, and books and towels were piled in loose stacks on the bed. Someone had pushed a rectangular table against the floor-to-ceiling window, and Zaffron stood behind it. His arms hung loosely at his sides as he looked out the glass, but when I entered the room, he turned to me, surprised.

"What are you doing here?" we spoke together. We stared at each other stubbornly, waiting for the other one to speak.

Zaffron's eyes shifted to the left, and I realized he was going to lie to me. As he opened his mouth, I interrupted him. "Don't lie."

His lips hung open in shock, holding his dishonesty on the edge of his tongue. Then his expression changed. "I'm spying on my father."

Those five words were enough to draw me in. "Namon? What is he doing?"

Zaffron sighed as if it took every ounce of his energy to remain civil. "He has been secretive, and I am trying to learn the reason."

I joined him at the window with my arms crossed. Zaffron tried to back me out of sight quickly, but he missed my shoulder and grabbed my breast. He jerked his hand away as if it had been shocked. "I didn't mean to. I was only going to—"

I saved him from his embarrassment. "It's okay." I backed away two steps. "Is this good?" From my vantage point, I could see the dirt road that led to Main Street. A couple of teachers parked their cars along the sides of it, but their vehicles were as empty as the road.

"I apologize for my mistake," Zaffron returned formally. "And, yes, you shouldn't be seen from where you are standing."

I thought about my misgivings about Namon. "Why do you think your father is doing something wrong?"

Zaffron brought his fist to his mouth and rested his elbow on his other arm. "He hasn't been the same since the day the talisman started losing power. My mother and I have seen less of him, and he is hardly ever in his office when I'm at school, yet he has used his work here as an excuse for his absence at home."

I felt like I was standing on dangerous ground. I had my doubts about Namon, but Zaffron was his son. Even though he may suspect his father now, it wouldn't mean he would bring the information to the council or confront his father with it. I decided to play it safely, and I asked him, "What have you learned?"

He scanned me, skeptically at first, but then approvingly. "I think he's sending messages to King Kano."

My mouth popped open, and I closed it quickly. Still treading carefully, I chanced another question. "How do you know?"

As if on cue, a blue Oldsmobile chugged up the dirt road. We watched it turn around in the grass, facing the exit.

Minutes later, Namon appeared. There was something in his hand, but I couldn't see it clearly. I leaned over to watch the exchange better, but Zaffron held up his hand. He didn't want to risk touching me inappropriately again, but his gesture warned me I might be seen if I moved closer to the window.

"Dragons have expert vision," he reminded me. He barely breathed the words.

The meeting was brief, and soon the Oldsmobile clattered back down the road. Zaffron wrote down the numbers on the car's license plate.

"How are you going to see who owns the car?" I asked.

"I have a friend who will find it out," he assured me, stuffing the paper into his leather pants.

I was impressed. Dragons and griffins usually didn't get along, and griffins were the only beings with access to that kind of information.

A door clanged and rattled. "It's my father," Zaffron whispered.

I panicked, looking around the room for a place to hide. Before I could dive under the table, Zaffron grabbed me from behind, placing a hand over my mouth. He backed into a corner with me and extended his wings, encircling us.

If anything, I thought his shift would make us more conspicuous, but Namon's footfalls continued to thud down the hallway without glancing into the slant window on the door.

Zaffron held onto me a little longer than I thought was necessary, but his quick thinking had prevented our discovery. His body felt warm and firm behind me, and I grew curious about whether he had to work out to build the rigid lines of muscles I felt through his shirt.

He lifted his hand from my mouth but kept his arm around my waist. His hot breath tickled my ear when he whispered, "I think he's gone."

I couldn't bring myself to move, but after he spoke, he released my waist and slipped from behind me. His wings retracted.

"I didn't know you'd started to shift." I wished my words sounded less shaky than they came out.

He smirked, and I reminded myself why I didn't like him. "Dragons evolved faster than the other species in our world. You should be glad of it since my wings made you invisible."

"Fayries evolved faster than—" I started to argue, but I stopped myself when I realized Zaffron had revealed a dragon secret to me. *Had he meant to trust me, or had he slipped?* I decided to press him and see if he truly meant to tell me the information. "Your wings make you invisible?"

He stuffed his arms into the leather jacket he had discarded before his shift. His shirt had holes for his wings, but his jacket was unblemished. "Yeah. Only if I wrap myself in them, though."

I looked around the room and thought about what to say next. "Do you come here every day?"

He made a show of making sure everything was in its place, straightening the already perfectly folded towels. "Almost. I try to watch my father's mouth move to see if I can make out plans."

"Have you learned anything?"

"Yeah, I found out—" He stopped speaking and studied me. I saw a flicker of light in one of his pupils. He walked to the door and held it open for me. It was more of a demand than a kind gesture.

I walked through the door and waited until he was in the hallway with me. He dismissed me, but I wanted to learn more about what Namon was doing. "I guess I'll see you here tomorrow unless you have other plans."

He put his head down as if he accepted my statement but then spat, "I don't need your help."

I took his sudden temper in stride. "That's fine, but I can read lips."

He stopped as if suddenly realizing I was a werewolf, but then he shook his head. "I need to do this myself."

"Everyone can use a little help sometimes." It was almost like the cliché had been planted on my lips by someone else, but it struck a chord with him.

Zaffron didn't look at me, but I could tell he had given in. "Meet me at the south barrier at midnight tonight. I think my father made plans for another exchange."

—•—

CHAPTER 15

I thought I might be crazy. Why else would I be standing at the south barrier at midnight, freezing in my long-sleeved shirt and jeans? It could be a trap, or Zaffron could have misled me so I would leave him alone.

Just as I was certain I'd been duped, I felt a warm hand on my waist. His touch steadied me, and I focused on the rough patch of grass where he pointed.

A dark figure hovered at the barrier. Lights flashed, and minutes later, two white-robed figures glided to a break in the glass. At first, they didn't see Namon, but when he passed them a paper through the dome, they nodded. The druids spoke, and I cataloged their words in my mind.

I shivered, and Zaffron stepped behind me, the heat from his body coming off him in waves. Warmth spread over me more evenly than if he had offered me his jacket.

Usually, werewolves had a body temperature higher than most beings. It surprised me that my internal thermometer was different from my peers.

In the moments that followed, I tried to concentrate on the humming of insects and the yellow-tinged grass. Zaffron finally moved. "I don't think we were noticed." He started walking, and I followed him.

"I'm going in the other direction," I announced when we got to the road.

He nodded his head but said nothing.

I grew frustrated with his apathy. "Did you see what they said?" I asked him.

"I couldn't make it out," he admitted.

I told him, "The druid thanked your father for his information. He said, 'I'll get your message to the right place.'"

Zaffron veiled whatever he was feeling behind a curtain of dark hair that slung across his profile. His severe nose inched up a notch before he cleared his throat and kicked one of his leather boots against the asphalt. After an uncomfortable moment, where I didn't know whether I should try to comfort him or walk away he said, "Goodnight, Corryne of Tribe Werewolf."

It was a formal and final farewell. It wasn't the way friends parted.

I stormed down the street. I was confused by Zaffron's actions, and I felt stupid for trying to help him. What's more, his father was passing messages to the descendants of the druids who had killed my ancestors, and I didn't know if Zaffron planned to do anything about it.

My house was half-covered by the night, but I could see the blonde in Allistar's hair as it reflected the moonlight. I inched down the side of my house and watched him tap my bedroom window.

"What brings you here?" I leaned against the wall next to my room and crossed my arms casually.

Allistar jumped and let out a shriek. Alarmed, I reached out for him, but he moved away before he realized it was me. His hand went to his chest. "What the—"

"I thought you were here to see me." I chuckled when he brought me into a hug. "I didn't expect you to cry out."

Allistar didn't deny his reaction. "You were supposed to be *inside* your house. What are you doing out here?"

I had a split second where I considered telling him the truth, but I worried he might tell someone who would alert Namon. I didn't want Namon to find out what Zaffron and I were doing.

"I walked outside for some fresh air." I tested my window, and finding it unlocked, I pushed it open and climbed inside.

Allistar looked at me skeptically. "Why didn't you go in your front door?"

My foot slipped, but I recovered quickly. "How would I be able to sneak you through the door?"

Allistar was diverted from asking more questions when I covered his mouth with my lips. He climbed through the window without unlocking our connection. I didn't want him to stay again, but we kissed until we fell asleep in each other's arms.

My mother's piercing screams woke us.

—·—

CHAPTER 16

"A unicorn!"

My father tried to calm her, but my mother continued to pace the length of the dining room.

I sat at the table with my head in my hands. Allistar had tried to bolt out the window, but my mother had grabbed him by the back of his shirt collar and thrown him out of the house properly.

My mother's shrill voice rang out again. "I guess I know why Rymon hasn't been here lately!"

My father grabbed my mother's shoulders to stop her. "Calm down, Maureen. Corryne says she only kissed him, and I believe her. The lineage remains intact."

I jumped up and shoved my chair under the table. "Is that all you two care about? Lineage?"

My mother glared at me. "If your grandfather were here—"

"He is," I spat. "My spiteful, vengeful, prejudice grandfather *is* here, and I see him in everything you do!"

I blazed into my room and slammed the door. My mother and father shouted at me from the other side of the door, but I ignored them and took a shower. When the water stopped running, the house was silent, so I assumed my father had dragged my mother to the dining room table to calmly discuss my punishment.

When I was ready to go to school, I marched right past my parents with my nose slightly elevated. It may have been childish, but I didn't want to make eye contact or speak to them again before I left.

Out of the corner of my eye, I noticed my father's drooped posture. "We'll talk about this when you get home."

I didn't glance in the direction of Rymon's house as I marched down the street. Overall, I didn't have the moral high ground, but my parents' prejudices bothered me. Why did they refuse to recognize love unless it was something their parents and the council told them was right?

I halted my thoughts, realizing that I'd thought about love. Did I love Allistar?

I had very deep feelings for him, and I was willing to change my genetic makeup to be with him, so I supposed it was true. Shouldn't I feel more tingly if it was love, though?

I thought about my parent's relationship. It had been over thirty years since they had taken vows, but they were happy. They obviously loved each other, but they didn't get goofy-eyed over it.

"Corryne!" a voice called. Fiona ran to catch up to me.

I looked around for her twin or boyfriend, but she was alone. As if reading my mind, she explained, "They're walking down the next road." She tilted her head in the direction of the next block.

I understood what she meant. Fallyn, Pat, and Puck didn't want to be seen with me.

"You should go catch up with them," I voiced in her direction. I didn't want her to walk with me out of pity.

"I think I'll hang out with you," she said. "If it's all the same to you."

"Whatever," I shrugged, pulling my hood over my head. I wrapped my arms around myself.

"I've noticed the dip in temperature, too."

I glanced over at her. Of course she had noted the change. She'd probably documented it in her science journal and experimented.

"It's not getting better."

"Well, according to the unicorns and vampires, the dome is receding, so I guess it's not going to get any better," I commented bleakly.

She laughed suddenly. "I know about the opening, Corryne. Everyone's been talking about the rain that poured on the vampire neighborhood.

I stopped and stared at her. "It actually rained on them?" I pointed up. "Like, from the outside."

She nodded. "Ledot was livid!"

I resumed my pace. "You know what that means. If the rain can get in, then the UV light from the sun can shine on them."

She kicked her leg out as she walked, looking at her pointy-tipped shoe. "Yep! A lot of them have relocated into the Forbidden Zone."

We neared the school, and I told her to go ahead of me. Fiona stubbornly stayed by my side, and we walked through the double doors. We were greeted by smirks and snorts, but we held our heads up.

I spent most of the day thinking about the change that had already affected our town. I spent the other half wondering about Allistar and if he was thinking about me.

— · —

CHAPTER 17

It was hard for me to remain indifferent to Namon when I passed him in the halls at school. I stared straight ahead as his soot smell billowed out when he passed me.

There were times when I thought I almost caught him looking at me as if he were measuring an opponent before a battle. I did my best to seem indifferent. I'd had a lot of practice watching my class-mate's demeanors as they drifted from class to class, flushing the material they learned and ignoring their surroundings. For mythical creatures with special powers, most of my peers were unobservant.

I slipped up to the room with Zaffron almost every school day. We had a study period after lunch, and it was easy to lie to the disinterested troll who watched over the class. When we told her we were finishing an assignment in the library for another class, she nodded without looking at us.

The more time I spent with Zaffron, the more conflicted I became about him. In our classes, he was cold and distant, but when I was alone with him, he was considerate and kind. One day, he asked me a surprising question.

"What would you do if you were in charge of the beings under the dome?"

We had been sitting cross-legged on the rectangular table in front of the window. The Oldsmobile hadn't made an appearance, and it was doubtful we'd see it. The wall clock ticked like a tapping foot as he waited for my answer.

It took almost a full minute for me to answer, but when I did, I spoke with more force than I'd intended. "I'd stop hiding. I'd gather my army and meet my enemies head-on. I'd find a way to march into King Kano's kingdom, and I'd raze them to the ground."

Something about my last sentence shocked Zaffron. His eyebrows shot up and his lips parted before his face resumed a non-committed look.

"What?" I asked him, pressing him to reveal the reason for his reaction.

He faced out the window. "It's just the way you put it. You said *raze*, and that's a word I hear from dragons, not werewolves."

I didn't feel the need to explore my language. Recently, I'd been in Zaffron's company much more than I'd been around werewolves. Instead, I asked him, "How would you change things?"

He took a deep breath, and when I was sure he wasn't going to answer me, he spoke, "I like your idea of seeking them out for battle. The dome is failing, and our enemies know it, so why not take the battle to them? Hopefully, they have become complacent while we have been here, and we can run a sword into the belly of their king before they realize we have left our town."

Zaffron's fingers drummed the table, and when he realized what he was doing, he stopped. "There are only two real problems with our plan: First, we don't have an army, and the vampires are the only creatures who remember how to fight. And second, we don't know the terrain outside this dome." He turned his hand over, palm up. "Well, except the vampires, but they probably aren't familiar with King Kano's kingdom."

"It's underwater," I reminded him.

He shrugged. "It doesn't matter to the undead. I'm sure a lot of them have been to Marilla, or they may have explored it before King Kano usurped the throne."

"Where is Marilla?"

"The mermaid's capital city is well hidden," he replied. "The griffins claim to know its location, but their information is outdated."

We sat in silence until it was time for our next class. Before we merged into the busy hall, he touched my arm. "It would be an honor to fight beside you."

My mouth dropped open as he brushed past me, his smell winding into my senses and sending bubbles into my stomach. I stayed back another moment, pondering his words. If we fought, all the beings under the dome would gather, but the dragons would fly while werewolves stayed on the ground. The only way Zaffron and I could fight side-by-side would be if I were a dragon, or if he changed into a werewolf.

—•—

CHAPTER 18

Curious notions swirled around my mind on my way home that afternoon. *Was Zaffron considering a life as a werewolf?* Perhaps he had thought of changing into another ground creature. I shook my head. If he was going to alter his origins, a werewolf was the closest being to a dragon in beliefs and traditions.

My eyebrows came together. Zaffron had always been a proud dragon, though. His assertion only made sense if he was trying to escape the shame of his father's actions.

An arm rested casually on my shoulder, and I slung it off before I registered its owner. "What do you want?" I shouted.

Allistar held his hands up. "Are you mad?"

I narrowed my eyes. We were on a lone patch of unoccupied road between neighborhoods. The street was quiet, except for chirping birds and noisy insects. "I haven't seen you in two weeks!" I seethed.

"Yeah, about that," he began, dropping his hands. "I've been doing some research."

I stood with my arms crossed. "You never did research in school. How am I supposed to believe—"

He interrupted me. "Look, after your mom kicked me out, I knew I'd have to find a way to be with you."

The ice in my heart started to melt. Allistar sensed it and smiled.

"Will you let me take you somewhere?" he urged. "It's not far."

I smirked and glanced around the strict confines of the dome. "Sure. But I need to be back before dark. My parents grounded me after they found me with you."

"You're still grounded?" he asked, lifting his arm to put it over my shoulder and placing it back at his side when I scowled at his effort.

"Yes," I answered. "Some parents have rules and consequences for not following them."

It was a low jab. Allistar's parents probably had rules, but their jobs kept them from enforcing them.

Allistar took my hand and ushered me over to a line of bushes. He lifted a patch of branches, and a well-worn path wound into the trees. I allowed him to hold my hand, but it was mostly out of fear as we entered the muted light of the forest. The vampire's neighborhood bordered this section of trees, and I wondered if any of them were stalking the woods, looking for a meal.

I had only been back in the Forbidden Zone a couple of times since my experience in the lake. There were moments when I could see the lake through the trees, the reflection of the sun glinting off its waters.

We walked almost a mile before Allistar stopped me and crouched behind a bush. I leaned into him, happy to be enveloped by his strawberry scent.

Beyond the bushes, a clearing stretched. Pink and purple flowers dotted the spring-green grass. A unicorn lifted his magnificent head and shook his silvery mane. It was clear he had just returned from a gallop; his body shone with the dew of his sweat.

As we watched, he returned to his human form, transitioning gently. I averted my eyes as he dressed in clothes he had thrown onto a nearby thicket.

We walked behind him, carefully hiding behind trees. He stopped at a wooden cottage with a severely square porch and thatched roof.

A woman opened the door and greeted him. She was blond and thin, with dark eyes and a small nose. She was human.

Before I could register my shock, Allistar darted out from behind the tree and dragged me with him. He approached the couple—and to my amazement—they smiled at him.

"Allistar!" the unicorn said, clapping him on the back. "What brings you to our neck of the woods?"

Allistar nudged me forward, even though I tried to hold my ground.

"Hey, Macon," Allistar said. "I'd like you to meet Corryne."

CHAPTER 19

"But you're a unicorn," I said lamely.

Macon humored me. "Yes, I'm a unicorn, but I found a beautiful mate"—he turned to his companion— "and I never looked back."

"Did you lose your powers?" I asked.

He glanced at Allistar and ushered us into his house. He made a grand gesture. "Mi casa, es su casa."

Allistar and I sat across from Macon and his partner after she gave us a drink that smelled strongly of blueberries. I was surprised when Allistar took my hand.

"I see why you're here." Macon nodded to our clasped hands.

Allistar leaned forward. "Do you think we can make it work?"

Macon held up his hand. "I think we need to start by telling our story to your young lady."

Allistar leaned back and put his arm over my shoulder. I moved against his side, happy for the chance to feel like a couple.

"This is my mate, Lily," Macon began, gesturing to the woman. "When he formed the dome, Archard drove out most of the humans. There were two families with special psychic powers who were unaffected by his spell.

"At first, they lived among us, disguising themselves as trolls to camouflage their smell. Unfortunately, it only lasted for a couple of decades. One day, Ledot felt compelled to enter the trolls' neighborhood. Her appetite brought her to a certain section of the woods, and she found the humans celebrating a recent union between their families.

"A slave to her nature, Ledot called to her kind, and they attacked the group. They massacred every human in moments, except for one. She hadn't been drinking, and she was more aware of her intuitions, so she ran away moments before the attack. She fled through the woods, masking her smell as she went. She ran away from the trolls' neighborhood and ended up in a shed behind my house.

"I found her three days later, scared and hungry. My family sheltered her, even though it was hard to keep her hidden."

Macon placed his hand on Lily's knee. "We were young, so neither of us felt the pull to one another until our teenage years. We planned our future in secret, hoping that we could be together."

I decided to be forthright, as I wasn't impressed by their love story. "She was a human virgin. Of course, you were drawn to her."

"I thought the same thing," Lily responded, her voice light and airy. "But Macon's affections didn't waver even after" —a blush dotted her cheeks as she searched for the right words— "our love was consummated."

Macon noticed his mate's embarrassment, and he made a playful remark. Her color deepened until I thought her red face might turn purple. After he had succeeded in making Lily flustered, Macon continued his story.

"At my Glistening, I inwardly begged the tree to sprinkle me with the dust of a purely human form, but I remained a unicorn. I was upset, and after returning home, I fought with my family. Lily and I ran away that night."

Lily looked at her lap. "Macon's family was good to me. I can't imagine what they thought of me after they learned we'd run away."

Macon lifted his wife's chin. "That was many years ago, and the time we've had has been full of love."

She smiled at him and placed her delicate hand in his rough one. "It still hurts to live invisibly."

"I'm sorry you have to hide," I said. "It seems like you're happy, though."

"We are," Macon agreed. "We'd be content here forever if it weren't for—"

Lily shook her head and demanded his attention. "No."

"But Allistar trusts her," he reasoned. "Why can't she know the rest of our story?"

"They're talking about me."

The voice came from the room across from them. Lily stood up as a boy about my age rounded the door. He had been listening to our conversation and had decided to reveal himself.

Lily sighed. "This is Robbie. "He's our son."

— • —

CHAPTER 20

It was hard for me to comprehend Macon's words. "You adopted him?"

Allistar shook his head. "Robbie is their natural-born son."

"But I thought—" I started. My eyes darted between Robbie and his parents.

"That's what we had all been told," Macon explained. "We were led to believe that we *couldn't* interbreed, but it seems like the council only wanted us to think that."

Robbie settled onto a chair perpendicular to the loveseats where we sat. He had his father's silver-blond hair, but his mother's dark skin tone and crystal blue eyes accentuated his features.

Macon patted his son's shoulder. "It turns out that other creatures can have offspring together, but their children's powers are weaker or nonexistent."

Lily's face creased. "Well, not every combination yields offspring." In the excitement over Robbie's appearance, her statement was mostly ignored.

I had been staring at Robbie since he'd walked into the room. "Do you—"

"—have powers?" He finished my sentence for me. He wound one bony finger around another. "I can get glimpses of the future sometimes, but I can't change into another creature."

The realization almost took my breath away. "They don't want us to interbreed because the offspring wouldn't be as strong."

"You got it." Allistar's words were flat.

"But why does it matter?" I asked. "We're all stuck here anyway. Why should we worry if we have powers or not?"

"Our powers feed the talisman," Macon answered. "Archard has been gone for many years. It's *our* magic that keeps the barrier in place."

A thousand questions passed through my mind, but I settled on the one most pertinent to our conversation. "Do you think others have interbred and weakened its power?"

Lily sat down and took her husband's hand again. "That's our theory."

After her vague reply, I narrowed my eyes. "You're psychic, though. Can't you see what's happening?"

Macon answered the question for his wife. "She has visions that just pop into her head. She never knows when they're coming or what they'll mean."

Lily stared at me intently. "In your case, Corryne, I can see beings from different races swirling around you." One eyebrow rose quizzically. "You're not like other werewolves, are you? You see beyond the prejudice of your kind."

I could sense Allistar's eyes on me. "I have a lot of friends. Most of them are faeries," I blubbered, wondering if she could see my stolen moments with Zaffron.

"You won't hear me speak against diversity," Macon chuckled, holding up the hand that clung loosely to Lily's fingers.

Allistar stood up, stretching his arms above his head. "Are you ready?" he asked Macon.

"As I'll ever be," he responded.

Macon and Robbie each kissed Lily's cheek and she locked her worried eyes on them. "Be careful."

I stared at Allistar for an explanation, but he only beckoned me to come with them. I said my farewells to Lily and followed them.

Lily held me back as the rest of the group talked outside. She stared at me, and I thought I could see Zaffron and Rymon moving through her irises.

"A divided heart will shatter," she whispered. "And its shards will cut everyone around you."

I didn't know how to respond to her cryptic warning. She turned away from me and filtered into the living room, and I took the chance to join the men outside.

"Straight in a line, four paces left, and run one mile," Allistar directed.

I furrowed my brow. "Are we going to the Glistening Tree?"

Allistar nodded and darted out of sight, closely followed by Macon and Robbie. Robbie might not have been able to shift into a unicorn, but he kept pace easily with his father and Allistar in their human forms. I used my speed to catch up to them, and since they had left me behind, I passed them and arrived at the tree before them. I was winded, but I had a minute or two to catch my breath before they stopped in the clearing. I stood against a tree with a full view of the Glistening Tree when they came into view. I had made overtaking them appear effortless, and I was proud of myself.

Robbie walked up to the tree reverently, and it was clear to me we were there to witness his Glistening. "Doesn't it have to be activated or something?" he asked his father.

Macon chuckled. "No, son. You just walk under the branches, and the dust that rains on you should turn you into your true form."

"Do you think it'll work?" He addressed his father, but the question was meant for all of us.

Allistar answered him. "I wouldn't have suggested it to waste your time. You're seventeen. You're ready." He put his hand on Robbie's shoulder. "Why shouldn't you have the same opportunity as the rest of us?" He waved his thin hand at the Glistening Tree. "I'll be walking under it, too, but it won't be for another couple of months."

I joined them, walking Robbie to the point where the shade of the Glistening Tree stretched across the forest floor. "I'll walk under it on the same day as Allistar," I offered.

His wide eyes fell on me, fear pooling in their crystal blue depths. "Will it hurt?"

Macon laughed good-naturedly. "Not at all, son."

We stayed still while Robbie hesitantly stepped under the tree's shadow. He wound around the tree and emerged on the other side. Golden dust shimmered over his skin. It was as shiny as glitter and as small as sand.

"I'm still human," he remarked.

Macon sighed; his previous good mood was gone. "Then your true form is a human."

Allistar clapped him on the back. "Being human is good."

Robbie appeared skeptical and shot a glance at Macon. "I'm a failure."

Macon told him it wasn't true, but he made no effort to comfort Robbie. He walked to an oak tree and squatted, putting his head in his hands.

"I thought it would help him," Macon said miserably.

"Me too," Allistar agreed solemnly.

"How am I supposed to defend myself now?" Robbie asked. He was trying to hold it together, but drops of moisture had already appeared on his lashes.

"Humans have been guarding themselves for years," Allistar informed him. "They had guns, knives—"

"We don't have guns here," Robbie yelled, causing birds to fly up from a nearby bush. "And the knives—" He laughed without humor. "What am I supposed to do, fight mermen with my mama's potato peeler?"

We were mostly silent on the way back. In our defeat, the excitement had dwindled, leaving us without the energy to run, so we walked through leaves that had started to fall. Macon put his arm around Robbie, but they didn't speak to each other.

"It was a pretty tree," Robbie commented. "Was it always here?"

"It used to be in Faldonia," I told him. "The griffins guarded it, and everyone received a sprinkling at seventeen. Archard moved it here when he cast the spell that made the dome."

"But what about the beings on the other side of the dome? Do they have a Glistening Tree?"

"No," Allistar told him. "It's the only tree of its kind."

Robbie's eyebrows drew together. "Then how do they—"

"—turn into their true forms?" I finished. "The Glistening Tree is only a formality. Most of us don't need it."

"What about the ones on the outside who do need it?"

I shrugged. "I guess they hover somewhere between human and their counterpart, never truly fulfilling their destinies."

Robbie slowed his pace and brought his thumb to his teeth, biting the nail. "That's terrible."

I didn't consider Robbie's failed transformation before I spoke. "They can still shift a little, so they're mostly okay. Besides, they're the ones who tried to kill us."

"That was a long time ago," Robbie spat.

Macon cut his eyes at him, and Robbie's voice softened. "I just can't imagine other races of beings feeling the same way I feel right now."

I was embarrassed with the flippant way I had treated his questions. "I'm sorry. I had never considered their feelings, but there is good and bad everywhere, so it makes sense that some good beings have suffered over the years." Robbie glanced up, but he didn't speak, so I added, "I'm a werewolf, and part of our nature is brutal. It makes me insensitive sometimes."

He smiled wanly. "It's okay. I shouldn't have snapped at you." He let out a long, exaggerated sigh. "I'm human, I guess, and that's the way we handle things."

Allistar grabbed my hand and tried to lighten the conversation. "You did a good job going around the tree, bro. Most beings have a lesson before Glistening Day, but your dad must have explained it to you pretty well."

Macon and Robbie exchanged a glance. "It's pretty easy. You just go around one side and out the other."

Allistar chuckled. "Yeah. That's true. I had no idea which side to go around until I saw you do it."

"You've never been to a Glistening?" Macon asked.

"It's reserved for parents and their children," I replied.

"That's different than it was when I lived in the community," he remarked.

Lily was waiting on the porch. Expectation shone in her eyes until Macon shook his head, and she extinguished her smile.

We said our farewells to the family and followed the gently used trail to the unicorn neighborhood. Halfway there, Allistar stopped me. I looked up into his deep violet eyes, letting their starbursts light up the failing sunlight.

"We can be together." He spoke it like a promise he planned to fulfill and not as a possibility. He ran his hand down my back, and I shivered. He smiled at my response to his touch.

Taking his cue from my desire, he tugged me close to him until he was between a tree and me. He leaned down to kiss me, his hair brushing across my eyelids. My tongue danced against his, and time passed as I melted into him.

I thought he would be more experienced than me, but I matched his moves, almost anticipating them. Our long kisses and gentle caresses lasted until well into the night.

"Stay with me," he begged. "We can stay right here or go back to the Glistening Tree." His mouth tugged up on one side.

I laughed. "Woah, boy! We need to slow down. We'll have plenty of time for that."

He placed his hand against my cheek. "You never know. King Kano could attack us tonight."

I turned around, and my feet negotiated the steep path. "I doubt it," I called over my shoulder.

He reluctantly followed me, tugging at the back of my shirt. I resisted his playful attempts to stop again and make out. I wasn't angry with him anymore, but my parents were definitely going to ground me again.

"What are you doing here?"

Ledot's raspy voice pierced my ears and mind. She stood before me, but her words echoed like we were in a wind tunnel. I imagined it would be mesmerizing to humans, but it irritated other beings.

"We were out for a walk," Allistar spoke up. He seemed less affected by her voice.

"Curious place for a walk." She allowed a black bug to crawl onto her hand. "This hill has a fourteen percent gradient. I can imagine the two of you would prefer to engage in other amorous activities rather than expend your energy climbing it."

"I like to hike," I volunteered. My voice came out slurred from the vertigo I felt when Ledot spoke.

She smiled benignly. "Yes, I'm sure. Dogs like the woods."

"And blood-sucking leeches like the shadows!" I shouted. My damaged equilibrium started to give me a headache that began at my temples and stretched its tendrils to the center of my brain.

Allistar held his hands up. "Look, we're just trying to get back to my neighborhood. We aren't in your territory, so let us go on our way."

"I wouldn't dream of keeping you from your chosen destination." She stood in the middle of the path but beckoned us to pass on either side of her.

I was the first one to charge forward. I passed her easily. Allistar was more hesitant, turning to his side to slip past her. She held his eyes the entire time. "Unicorn blood is delicious," she mocked, her fangs touching her lower lip. "It tastes like sun-ripened strawberries in a field of flowers."

"We're not in your neighborhood," I reminded her.

"But this isn't anyone's neighborhood." She gestured at the wild forest around us. "I owe no tribute to these woods."

Allistar grabbed my hand, and we walked away. He wouldn't turn his back to Ledot, but I strode forcefully down the path. Still, both of us were relieved to see the opening that led into his backyard.

"What do you think she was doing?" I asked him.

He squinted when the streetlights washed over us. He had been holding my hand, but he dropped it and shoved his hands into his pockets. "They still have to hunt. They drink blood from bears, squirrels, and deer without fully draining the animals."

I scrunched up my nose. "That sounds gross. Do they ever kill anything?"

His shoulders peaked. "It probably happens once in a while, but they seem to be pretty careful. It's not like they have an unlimited supply of animals. They have to keep them alive and healthy enough to reproduce and have more animals."

"It sounds like a sad and disgusting cycle." I watched my feet pad against the pavement. "Why don't they try to drain us?"

"They could drink from you and you'd never know it." He cupped the side of his neck absentmindedly. "Truth is, Ledot could have drunk from both of us a few minutes ago."

"I think I would have noticed."

Allistar raised his eyebrows. "Maybe. Maybe not. How much do you remember about vampires from class?"

My palm smacked my head. "That's right! She could have hypnotized us."

"I prefer to think of it as altering our memories."

My fingers traced the place on my neck where I thought my jugular vein ran. "Do you think she fed on us?"

Allistar appeared thoughtful. "Probably not. I think she was having too much fun toying with us."

I had stayed out past my new curfew, but I wasn't worried. I only had a short time left in the house with my mother and father, and I could withstand their punishment as long as I knew Allistar would be waiting for me after my Glistening.

We reached the edge of the unicorn neighborhood and parted. I was surprised when he didn't try to lead me into the shadows to kiss me. When I asked him about it, he moussed the back of his hair and looked at the houses around us. "It's probably not safe right now."

I waved casually and walked the rest of the way to my house. I had just enough time to be angry that he hadn't offered to walk me home. We had already run into a vampire, and it was dark. *Weren't unicorns known for their chivalry?*

I talked myself out of my anger before I climbed my porch steps. Allistar may not want anyone to know about us now, but he went to all the trouble to track down a way we could be together. I was happy with the information I had learned, but I had a plan of my own, and it was almost time to set it in motion.

CHAPTER 21

My parents were incensed.

I didn't make it inside before my mother yelled at me. I walked backward as she advanced.

"You were with the unicorn," she shouted, pointing her finger at me. "Don't try to deny it; his scent is all over you!"

"I won't deny it," I spoke evenly, refusing to match her volume.

"I think it's time for you to leave." Her finger moved from inches away from me to the direction of my room. "Pack your stuff and get out!"

I fumbled for something to say. "I-I will."

"Stop it, Maureen," my father warned. "She's not of an age to—"

My mother rounded on him. "She can't be on her own, but you think she can defy our rules?"

My father held her eyes, but he didn't speak.

My mother snorted. "That's what I thought." She turned back to me. "If my father were alive, he'd banish you."

I rolled my eyes. "*Your father*?" I put my hands on my hips. "He's not my grandfather anymore?"

"He wouldn't be able to stand you," she snarled.

"That's fine," I returned. "He was part of the problem anyway. He couldn't see the beauty in another being unless they worshiped the moon!"

"GET OUT!" my mother bellowed.

"Wait!" A voice called out.

Rymon stepped out of the shadows, shocking everyone. My mother's mouth remained open, but her words were suspended on her tongue.

"Corryne was with me," he covered, taking another step into the moonlight. "We were helping our friends, and some of them were unicorns."

My mother finally recovered enough to speak. "I thought you were no longer friends with Corryne." Usually, my mother referred to me as her daughter, but she used my name. To some, the difference would be meaningless, but I understood the distinction. My mother was distancing herself from me.

Rymon shook his head. "Her dalliance was difficult to overcome, but she begged my forgiveness. I'm willing to move forward with our union."

My heart dropped somewhere into my stomach. My expression had to have been obvious, but my parents chose to ignore it.

"That's good news," my father said. "We value your family's company and lamented our daughter's mistake."

My mother's eyes narrowed. "Corryne is a blood traitor. Are you truly willing to forgive her?"

If it wouldn't have destroyed Rymon's lie, I would have exploded, unleashing my feelings on both of my parents. Part of me wanted to reconnect with Rymon, though, even though I didn't want to unite with him.

Rymon nodded. "She indeed disgraced herself with Allistar, but she was overtaken by his charms. He wooed her in a moment of weakness." He glared at me, putting extra emphasis on his next words. "But she's stronger now and sees the error of her ways."

My mother sighed. "I suppose I can look over her actions tonight if she has won your forgiveness."

"Corryne has my heart," Rymon almost whispered.

I believed him and felt like my heart had been squeezed in response to his declaration. I didn't want him to carry the weight of my rejection. He was my best friend and long-time confidant.

Rymon reached out his hand. I thought about my feelings for Allistar and the selfishness behind them. *What did I really expect to happen?*

Sure, I didn't totally fit with the werewolves' line of thinking. As a race, most of them were brash, vindictive, and ruthless to anyone outside their species. But... I had been born a werewolf. I was a

Lycan, and the Glistening Tree would respond to my request in much the same way as it did when Macon and Robbie passed under its branches. It wasn't there to honor my desires; the Glistening Tree was only meant to sharpen the abilities of my true form.

No matter how much I wanted to be with Allistar, I was stuck in my form, and our love wouldn't be tolerated because it was shared between beings from different neighborhoods. His kisses could melt me, and his laugh was musical, but we could never have offspring who were accepted. The idea of living in the forest, away from prying eyes, was appealing, but spending my nights in fear of vampire attacks and my days alone, did not fulfill my goals for my future.

If, however, I concentrated on being a werewolf, the world lay before me. I could choose any job I wished. My mother was a homemaker, as were most female werewolves, but it wasn't unheard of for a female to request a job placement just after her Glistening. I thought about the perfect position for me, and I arranged steps in my head to meet my goal.

All my thoughts passed through my mind in seconds. I stared at Rymon's outstretched hand, and I took it.

"I'm ready to start my future," I said. "And it is an honor to have Rymon by my side."

— · —

CHAPTER 22

I hopped onto the table next to Zaffron and peered out the window. He stared outside, watching for the Oldsmobile. We had seen it once that week, and it seemed like only verbal information passed between Namon and the unknown driver.

Zaffron had given the license plate number to his source, but the car wasn't registered to a known being under the dome. I thought about Macon and Lily and wondered if it might belong to someone like them.

"The leaves are already changing," Zaffron pointed out.

I followed his gaze to a proud maple tree. Its leaves had lightened to a pale yellow, and some had fallen around the base of the trunk.

I motioned to the rose-colored light that encased the dome, replacing the yellow rays that had filtered through the barrier before the talisman had been compromised. "The plants probably aren't getting enough heat. I hope the dome can be fixed soon."

Zaffron slapped his hand on the table, making me jump. "The *dome* is the problem!"

He spun around, pushed off the table, and paced the room, running a hand through his dark hair. "I thought we talked about it. You agreed that we should take our fight right to King Kano!"

I had said it, but I only meant it was better to take the fight to our enemies than for them to rain war onto us. "What good would it do? You and I are the only ones who seem to believe in that kind of campaign. How would the two of us measure up against an army of mermaids, elves, and druids?"

He stared at me, and I could almost see my reflection in his emerald eyes. There was something he wanted to say, but I wondered if he would say it.

"There are others." He whispered it into the still room.

My mind raced with possibilities and landed on obvious subjects. "Mantible and Nava?"

Zaffron lifted his upper lip. "Dragons are fiercely loyal."

That didn't answer my question. Either he meant Mantible and Nava were loyal to him or Naman. Their absence led me to believe it was the latter, and that meant Zaffron was convinced his father was a traitor if he was willing to defy him.

"The way I see it, Namon is the clear and present danger." I didn't reference him as Zaffron's father, so it made it easier for us to think of him as the enemy. "We need to destroy his credibility with the council so we can expose him as a traitor."

Zaffron nodded. "The only way to do that is by challenging him." His jaw clenched, and he spoke through his teeth. "I should do it."

I grabbed Zaffron's hand without thinking about it. The action was meant to be compassionate, but the way his eyes locked on mine made me feel like he thought it meant more. I dropped his hand and looked back out the window, color creeping into my cheeks.

My reaction only made the moment more awkward. Zaffron cleared his throat. "He won't kill me." He seemed sure and steady. "I'm his only son, so if he beats me, he won't deliver a death blow."

I couldn't see Naman as a forgiving being. "You said it yourself. Dragons are loyal. He'll know you don't agree with his actions, and your mother can produce another egg. You may think you're irreplaceable to him, but he can have another heir."

"That's not—" he started and didn't finish or try to change the subject.

"You have a prime spot to spy on him," I spoke. "You can watch what he does, but you won't be as effective if he knows you suspect him." I tapped my chin thoughtfully. "Who are the others?"

Zaffron shook his head, but I persisted.

"Do I know them?"

He nodded once and walked to the door. "You'd be surprised by some of the beings who want to stop hiding uselessly."

"Who are—"

Zaffron shushed me and held a finger to his lips. I sat motionless as he pressed his ear to the door. Footsteps echoed down the hall.

Most days, Namon breezed down the hall parallel to the room where we sat, but he had chosen to take another route one other time, causing Zaffron to conceal me with his wings. It seemed he was stomping down the hall, and he'd be able to see us easily through the rectangular window in the door, despite its size.

There was no time to hide. Zaffron couldn't have thrown off his jacket and extended his wings in the amount of time we had before Namon zipped past the room, his beyond-perfect eyesight locking in on any differences. I saw my panic momentarily reflected in Zaffron's features. He formed a plan in the time it took to blink.

Zaffron took four swift steps and wrapped me in his arms. When his lips met mine, they tasted like fire and salt water. I found that I liked the combination and surprised myself by exploring his mouth with my tongue. He sucked in a breath through his nose and pulled me closer, cradling my head with one hand and resting his other hand on my lower back. I was so lost in Zaffron's kiss that I forgot about the approaching danger, and I didn't want to break away when Namon opened the door and shouted at us.

"What is going on here?"

Most guys would have jerked out of the kiss and jumped away, but Zaffron eased away from my lips and continued to hold me. "Hello, Father. You may not remember it, but I'm sure you, too, were in love when you were young."

Naman snarled and spat. I was so shocked that I could only focus on the saliva on the floor.

Namon grabbed Zaffron by his arm. "Our house has not fallen so low that its members fraternize with dogs."

Zaffron shrugged him off with effort and stood between us. "I'm not going to let you speak about her that way."

Namon took two steps and breathed down on his son. A small cloud of smoke escaped his nose and billowed around him.

I was scared, so I did the only thing I thought could diffuse the situation. I ran away.

Walking home from school, I shook my head when I thought about my hasty escape. I should have stayed and stood up to Namon with Zaffron. *What did that say about me? Would I always turn my tail and run at the first sign of danger?*

I saw his shadow before I felt his arm around me. I was annoyed by his touch, but I leaned into him. There was no reason for me to be mad at my boyfriend, except that he had left me to my fate after my mom had kicked him out, and he hadn't walked me home in the dark when we had visited Macon and Lily.

The Glistening is six weeks away," he said. "Are you excited about becoming a unicorn?"

I shrugged my shoulders. "You know, you could always turn into a werewolf." Even as I said the words, I knew they were absurd, but I wanted Allistar to feel so strongly about me that he would consider it. Instead, he assumed I should be the one to change.

He raised his eyebrows, brushed in a fuchsia glitter, and dropped his arm.

I pushed on. "I mean, with the dome failing, and King Kano's threat, wouldn't it be better to be a being known for their fierce fighting skills?"

He chuckled and pointed to his forehead. "My horn can be pretty deadly. And if that doesn't do it, I still have my magic." We walked a few more paces before he spoke again. "Is that what's bothering you? Do you think we're going to be at war soon?"

I motioned to the crimson hues in our sky and the withering plants. "Don't you? It's only a matter of time before the dome fails, and we have to face whatever army our enemies have built."

Allistar looked at his feet and matched my pace. Our shadows looked sinister in the red light. "It's only natural to have second thoughts. You'll be leaving behind a lot."

"I know," I returned harshly. "That's why I think you should change instead of me. At least I have parents that care about me enough to be around."

He stopped short. At first, I kept walking, but then I realized I'd hit him way below the belt. I jogged back to him and noticed the casual swipes he made to his face to wipe away the tears he didn't want me to see.

"I'm sorry," I told him, taking his hand. He didn't pull away, but his hand was limp and held no warmth. "I've been under the protection of the dome my whole life, and now I have to worry about going into battle."

He seemed to understand. "Mariam's scared, too."

I sucked in a breath, and he realized what he had said. He fumbled for a defense and came up short.

"You're still talking to the human, aren't you?" Realization dawned on me, and I dropped his hand. "That's why you're out late at night. You leave her and come to my window."

I wanted him to deny it. I expected lies to fall from his lips that professed his fidelity, but he honored our friendship more than he cared for my feelings.

"I didn't plan for it to be this way." He wouldn't look at me, and I almost expected him to shift and gallop away. "Her parents took her away. It's never going to happen again."

"What's it? What will never happen again?"

He finally met my eyes. "Nothing. It was nothing."

"While we were together?"

He dropped his eyes again, and I had my answer.

"I think we need to break up."

I'd planned to break up with him after the Glistening. I had unofficially accepted Rymon's proposal, and his mother was already arranging a ceremony for our union, so I knew that my time with Allistar was drawing to a close. Selfishly, I had wanted to share the remaining days of my youth with Allistar, making out and looking into his violet eyes. But he had offered me a way out of the relationship that left me blameless, and I took advantage of it.

Allistar closed the distance between us in one swift motion. "No!" He held my hands to his chest. "Please, Corryne. You know about the pull between a unicorn and a virgin. I was powerless." He got on his knees in front of me. "But I promise, if you stay with me, I will make it up to you."

"Well, she's not a virgin anymore," I pointed out.

Tears were streaming down his face. "I know. And for me, the longing is gone, but she was given the gift of sight."

Before the dome was erected, human virgins who won the favor of a unicorn hadn't been rare. Unicorns fixated on at least one a week until they matured. Sometimes, though, the human would give herself to a unicorn, bestowing upon that being the gift of her virginity. In return, the flower of sight rested on their eyes, giving the humans skills like premonition or telekinesis.

Allistar was a slave to his kind, and I couldn't be angry with him. Who was I to judge the biology that made him a unique creature? After all, I was drawn to Allistar, and even though my heart was broken over his infidelity, I hadn't been truly faithful. I planned to take vows with Rymon, and I had kissed Zaffron. And if I was honest, the kiss I had shared with the dragon had rattled me.

I stared down into Allistar's mesmerizing violet eyes and accepted his apology. He was right; unicorns were powerless against the call of a virgin. I pulled his arms, and he got to his feet.

I didn't want to kiss him. I was a little nauseated when I thought about kissing him after he'd left Mariam's arms. Her family had taken her away, though, so Allistar was all mine now.

He leaned into me with a soft smile, and his silvery hair brushed my cheek. I breathed in the familiar scent of strawberries. When he put his hand on my lower back, I jumped, surprising both of us. It felt too much like the way Zaffron had held me when we'd kissed.

"I need to go home," I told him, slipping my silver streak behind my ear.

"Can I accompany you?" he asked for the first time.

I nodded my consent and walked the last two blocks in silence. He wasn't allowed inside my house, so we stopped under the shade of my neighbor's tree.

He kissed me, but I kept my mouth tightly shut. He licked his lips. "Have you been around a fire?"

I blushed and dropped my eyes. "We had a fire drill today."

"With a real fire?"

"Zaffron started it," I lied, pecking him on the cheek and jogging away before I could hear his response, or see the confused look on his face.

Maybe I had told a half-truth. It seemed like my kiss with Zaffron had sparked a fire of doubt in my mind.

— • —

CHAPTER 23

I was glad to be back in my parents' good graces, and my mother's attitude toward me had improved. She brightened when Rymon came over to see me before school and pressed me to hold his hand as we ate breakfast.

It was hard to have the use of only one of my hands, and Rymon seemed uncomfortable with it, too. His occasional looks at me expressed his amazement over my mother's request, but he didn't deny the opportunity to be closer to me.

With his declaration of love, I thought my parents would be stricter about the time I spent with him alone, but they encouraged it. Not only was Rymon still allowed to go into my room, but he could lie on my bed for hours with the door closed. During those times, I would sit at my desk, even though he asked me to lie down with him. His request was harmless, as I had no intention of allowing his advances, but I thought it was best to build our friendship again before we took vows.

It was hard to pretend to be happy at school. I didn't have to worry about Allistar looking at me as I held Rymon's hand and accepted the kisses he placed on my cheek, but my friends seemed to judge me at varying levels.

One day, as I walked away from my last class of the day, Fiona followed me. She grabbed my arm, expecting me to stop. I slowed my pace, but I didn't want a good portion of the school to speculate on our conversation. Reading my intentions, she waited until we breached the doors of the school.

"What's going on?"

I clenched my jaw. Leave it to a faerie to be presumptuous.

I decided not to play ignorant. "I don't owe you an explanation."

"You don't," she agreed. "But I'm concerned about you."

I rounded on her. I had been closer to Fallyn than I had been to her, but I had never really shared a lot with them.

"Why?" I barked. She jumped, and I dialed back my tone. "Why do you want to know anything about what's going on?"

"I thought we were friends," she muttered under her breath.

I had no intention of burning any more bridges. I'd felt the loss of Rymon's friendship acutely, and I wasn't ready to lose another confidant.

"We are friends," I conceded, gritting my teeth. "What do you want to know?"

"You don't love Rymon, so why are you going to take vows with him?"

I had expected her to be a little less obvious, but I liked her straightforwardness. It prompted me to give her an honest answer.

"It's expected."

"I can understand that." She dipped her head, staring at the sidewalk.

I'd never considered that other beings were unhappy with their betrothed. Everyone seemed glad to be paired with someone, and I thought I was the only one who had misgivings about aligning myself with someone when the primary foundation of our relationship was that we were of the same race.

"You don't love Pat?" I almost breathed out the words in my shock.

She shook her head and looked up quickly. "Please don't tell Fallyn! She thinks we're going to marry twins and have twins at the same time."

"Do you have someone you favor?"

We started walking again, more comfortable in each other's company.

"Not really," she answered. "I don't want to take vows right now." She pointed up at the ruby sky. "It seems like we should be concentrating on other things."

"I know." I struggled to find the words to explain myself and settled on the most basic feelings. "I have conflicting beliefs on love, but I'm one hundred percent certain that we shouldn't be cowering behind what's left of the dome. I think we should be focusing less on traditions and more on organizing a strategy to take on King Kano."

"I'm sure he's not been complacent."

It was refreshing to hear my friend echo my thoughts. I had freely voiced my concerns with Zaffron, but I didn't know if he was rebellious because of his father's misconduct or because he truly believed in the cause. When Fiona spoke, though, I felt validated.

"I'd be surprised if there wasn't a force of elves just outside the dome's borders." She glanced up at the receding structure. "Right now, the very top of it is gone, but we don't know how fast it'll reveal the town or if we'll wake up tomorrow with it crumbling around our heads.

I grabbed her hand. "I have an idea."

Fiona raced down the road with me without question, and when we entered my neighborhood, several of my neighbors gave us furtive glances. I glared at them, never letting go of her hand.

CHAPTER 24

Lycon didn't look up from the book in his hand as we entered, reminding me of a time when Rymon and I had visited him. This time, however, he was already in his blue chair, holding the book Cyprus had written.

"To what do I owe the pleasure of your company?" came his familiar greeting. "It's not often that I receive such lovely visitors."

Some may have viewed his comment as creepy, but I knew its direction. He wanted Fiona to know that—even though she was a fayrie—he did not share the beliefs of his kind, and she was welcome in his home. He motioned to the loveseat nearest him, and we sat down together.

"We're here about the dome," I told him. "Do you know what's happening to it?" He raised his eyebrows, and I clarified my meaning. "We know it's disappearing, but we want to know WHY it's happening."

He sucked in a sharp breath. "I have a theory." He tightened his grip on the book he was holding. "I believe the dome is failing us because we have failed each other."

I hadn't expected his explanation. I had thought he would give us a more practical reason—like someone pushed a button, and the glass structure started retracting.

We waited for him to go on. He stared back at us, expecting us to fill in the blanks.

I was the first to speak. "Werewolves don't generally like other creatures, but some of us aren't like that."

His lips flew up in the corners. "Yes, but that was similar to the atmosphere before we fled to beg Archard for refuge. When we arrived, lines were drawn, and groups were formed."

"We can't even live in the same neighborhoods," Fiona added. "Even now, existing in something that could have been a utopia, we have areas designated to certain kinds, and specific supernatural creatures are assigned stereotypical jobs, like the way your kind" —she pointed between Lycon and me— "are either teachers or landscapers, and unicorns work in cosmetology or healing."

Lycon pointed at her. "You make a good point, Fiona."

I was surprised he knew she wasn't her sister. People mistook them all the time, even when they styled their hair differently.

"We should have come together as a community, working to preserve our kinds. Instead, we worked in separate areas, hardly ever combining our being-power or resources."

I nodded at his wise words. "We need to band together and prepare to fight."

Lycon's eyes went wide. "We could never hope to overcome the army that awaits us."

My breath caught in my throat. "What are we to do then? Are we supposed to wait for them to overtake us?"

"We must run," he answered, then shrugged. "Well, those who can run should flee beyond the reach of the mermaid king."

"Is there such a place?" Fiona asked him.

He shook his aging head. "No, sweet child, he will find us wherever we go. We'll have to scatter like seeds in the wind, each drifting, but never planting ourselves in the soil."

Life as a refugee was unappealing, and I told them how I felt about it. "I plan to stand and fight."

"Then you will die," he responded simply.

"Then I will die on my feet instead of cowering in the corner," I responded with my nose climbing higher. "Besides, I'm not the only one who will rise against his oppression," I countered.

"And how large of a group will you gather?" He scoffed. "You should have seen the massacre when we fought against them last time. My brethren fell to the left and right of me with steel-tipped arrows in their bellies, and one barely missed me." His eyes were glassy with tears. "You can't bring back the ones you love when they're gone."

I reached out and grabbed his hand. He allowed me to hold onto him, but he didn't squeeze my hand or look at me as I talked.

"Please help us," I pleaded. "You have so much knowledge about other creatures, and we'll need it when the dome disappears."

His mirthless laugh echoed in the still room. "As soon as the dome is accessible by repelling, you will see a league of elves cross into our borders."

"Are you giving up?" I asked softly.

His mouth settled into a grim line. "I'm not ready to die, but King Kano's soldiers will seek me out."

"Why?" Fiona voiced.

A knock at the door startled all of us. I almost wondered if the elves were already at Lycon's door, ready to take him to King Kano. The visitor didn't enter, so Lycon flipped on a small device next to his chair. The mystery of how he knew the identity of his visitors before they entered his home was solved, as an image of the being on his porch appeared.

"Rymon?" I hadn't meant to speak his name aloud.

Lycon stared at the monitor quizzically. "He visits often, but he usually lets himself inside."

With little effort, he pushed himself off the chair and jogged to the door. I expected muffled voices, but when no sound came to my expert ears, I raised my eyebrows at Fiona. She understood my concern and shrugged.

It took Lycon several minutes to return from answering the door. When he came back into the room, he appeared graver than when he'd left it.

Rymon followed him and addressed me as soon as he saw me. "You need to come with me. There's something I have to show you."

I didn't want to abandon Fiona, but Rymon insisted I follow him alone. We walked in silence, even though I wanted to prod him for information.

I let him guide me by my hand, and it felt more friendly than romantic. Rymon had something on his mind, and it pushed down his need to claim me as his own.

We walked away from our community and through the faeries' area. Colorful cottages sprang up on either side of the road with swing sets, trampolines, and swimming pools within view. The fayries had multiple children at a time, and they cared for them in much the same way as human parents had reared their children before the dome was created. Their offspring were treasures, and the parents cherished their time with their progeny.

Trolls had a similar upbringing, but they were taught to be modest. Bredek was almost as smart as Fiona, but he was too humble to let everyone know it.

At the edge of the fayries' bounds, Rymon took a sharp right, placing us in front of a line of maple trees. Their leaves were golden and sunset and drifted lazily to our feet.

"Do you know where we are?" Rymon asked.

"Of course," I answered. "I'm the one who took you here the first time."

He pulled me between the two tallest trees and led me to a road that had once been a more heavily traveled street. The area wasn't part of the Forbidden Zone, but it wasn't used by any of the tribes. No one cared for it, so the underbrush from the forest had crept over the road and wrapped around some of the buildings.

I had found the area accidentally while I had been playing a game with Fallyn and Fiona. I had hidden from them in the first house, a white two-story with an attached garage. When they didn't find me, I explored the home, finding dirty plates and bowls that had mildewed in the sink and closets full of clothes. I tried a few of them on before I noticed the holes the moths had chewed into them.

After I'd toured one old house, I wanted to see more, so I popped back in to finish my game with Fallyn and Fiona. They'd wondered where I had hidden, but I didn't tell them about the secret place I'd found. I ran home and noticed Rymon on his porch. Once I told him about the relics in the house, he followed me there the next day.

We looked through each room, discovering trinkets and toys. Some hadn't aged well, but others, like a metal train engine Rymon found, looked like they could go in a shop window after he dusted it off.

Rymon took his prize when we walked off the squeaky porch, and we stared down the road. The property next to us was free of a house, but there was a driveway leading to a place where a foundation had been dug and had grown over with spring green grass. I was drawn to the area, and I stepped right up to the driveway.

Lines for hopscotch and races had been drawn on the asphalt, and the chalk was so dark that it could have been done earlier that same day. I bent down and touched the blue, pink, and yellow lines, and when I brushed my hands across them, they didn't smudge.

I wasn't certain how long Rymon and I stared at the driveway, but the sun was low in the sky before we decided to go home. Rymon still had the train engine on a shelf in his room, and even though it was out in full display, his parents never asked him any questions about it.

As we walked past the white house, I noticed very few changes, but I had visited at least once a week since I'd discovered the place. I knew every building, tree, and moss-covered stone by heart. It was almost like walking into my living room and seeing the furniture arranged in the same way.

Except for this time, something was different. The trees still crowded the houses, and the weeds were thick, but another home stood proudly at the end of the driveway where I had often sat.

A beautiful Victorian house with maroon siding and large windows was positioned at the end of the chalked driveway. It seemed as if it had been there for years, but its structure was in much better shape than the houses that surrounded it.

Some of the windows were open, and a few of them had been broken. Sheer curtains flipped in an upstairs window, but I couldn't feel a breeze.

"I come here a lot," Rymon admitted.

I stared at him, surprised. "I do, too, but I didn't see the house the last time I was here."

"Me either," he agreed. "As far as I know, it showed up today."

I didn't waste another moment. I bolted to the door, leaving Rymon outside.

CHAPTER 25

A rush of air met me when I opened the heavy wooden door. It wasn't air conditioning, but it was like several fans were directed into the room, circumventing the airflow but not adding coolness.

I stopped for a moment, unsure of the best direction to begin my search. *Search for what?* I didn't know, but I was ready to find whatever treasures the house had to offer.

I turned left into what appeared to be a study or library. A medium-sized wormy chestnut desk had been scooted to the window, and a red velvet couch was next to the door. Blood covered the lower part of the couch, but it seemed to have dried a long time ago.

I walked over to the desk, and my eyes fell upon a blueprint for the dome that housed us. Inside it, happy supernatural creatures held hands as dragons and unicorns flew over them. Whoever had drawn it had imagined a perfect life for those placed in its confines.

"It's crazy, isn't it?" Rymon asked.

I jumped and held a hand over my heart. He walked over and tapped the blueprint.

"He drew this in a matter of hours," Rymon told me. "And he conjured up enough magic to erect it, even though he was under a tremendous amount of pressure."

We stared at it reverently.

"Do you realize we probably wouldn't be here without this dome?"

He nodded along. "King Kano may not have been able to find every mythical creature, but he would have picked off the ones he could find until entire races of the beings who opposed him were eliminated."

"Why did you go to Lycon's house?" I asked.

"To try to find you," he answered.

I put my hand on his wrist. "No, Rymon, why do you go there? Lycon told Fiona and me that you visit regularly."

He gave me a sheepish grin. "Well, at first, I liked the train set, but then I started to talk to him about other things, like the lack of equality and certain expectations."

"What kind of expectations?" I hoped he would mention our betrothal. It would be the perfect way for me to get out of it without letting him down and losing his friendship forever.

"I'm supposed to be a teacher, but I want to be part of the police force," he said, dashing my hopes. "Your brother was able to sneak into a position, but it's very rare for a werewolf to join."

The police force was largely dominated by griffins and vampires, and no fayries or unicorns had ever been permitted to join the ranks. I was also slated for a teaching position as I had turned down the opportunity to follow in my mother's footsteps. Homemaking was great for those who liked it, but I craved more adventure.

"I know it's hard," I consoled him. "Remember, though, you aren't the only one who has to fall into the positions others choose for you."

"I know," he bit back, and I withdrew my hand. "Everyone thinks I'm a dumb dog who can't make my own decisions."

"That's not true, Rymon. Most of us have our positions chosen for us. You aren't the only one who has to work in a job they don't want." I wanted to add that he wasn't betrothed to a mate he didn't love, but I decided to keep most of my hostility to myself.

I took a deep breath and tried another approach. We were friends, and I had been miserable without him, so I wanted to drive away animosity.

"I'm glad you have spoken with Lycon. He's always been a good source of wisdom."

I thought back on my last conversation with Lycon and I regretted my words. I didn't support his feelings about running and hiding from our enemies, and I wondered why he was so scared of them. From what I had read, merpeople lived long lives but could be killed. The elves were the supernaturals who concerned me the most. They were similar to vampires in longevity, but they fed off nature instead of sucking life from living beings.

"I like Lycon, but he's weak."

Rymon hadn't been present for my last conversation with our leader, but he echoed my thoughts. Beforehand, I would have argued with him. Lycon had been known as a skilled fighter, but something had weakened his spirit.

I turned my attention back to the blueprint. Rymon followed my gaze.

"There's nothing written on it that tells why it's not working anymore."

I studied the drawing, but it yielded no results. I picked up some of the smaller books around it, and my eyes fell upon a curious title.

"This says it's a book about werewolves."

Rymon edged closer to me. "I've not seen anything about us before."

I tapped the cover. "I've read little swatches of information in collections, but I've never seen a volume dedicated to our kind."

"Not even the members of our species want to write about us."

I nodded my head. "Lycon has a book that Cyprus has written, but I think it's more about the dome than it is about anything else."

"Yeah," Rymon agreed. "I used to look at it but didn't really understand it."

I gasped. Lycon hadn't allowed me to borrow the book, but he had let Rymon read parts of it. I was angry until it occurred to me that he probably would have let me read it, too, as long as I hadn't taken it out of his house.

"Do you remember anything about it?"

Rymon picked up some other books before tossing them back onto the table after reading their titles. "Not really. There was a lot of stuff about unityUn and the power behind it."

I rolled my eyes. Maybe it was better that I hadn't read Cyprus's book.

I flipped past the title page and ran my finger down the table of contents. "It says there are sections on werewolf anatomy, occupations and skills, and..." I trailed off, not sure of the best way to read the next section aloud.

"Werewolf reproduction!" Rymon laughed, elbowing me in the side. "I guess we'll be learning about that part soon."

I gave him an uncommitted smile.

He scanned the rest of the page. "Hey, what's this?"

I glanced at the area where his thumb had landed. "About a Werewolf and Dragon Union," I read aloud.

Rymon's eyebrows waggled.

"Rymon!" I admonished. "It's not a guide on how to have sex with a dragon!"

"How do you know?" He thumbed through the pages until he landed on the appropriate section.

Since the middle ages, Lycans and vampires are bitter foes, but there is a frequently ignored enemy and curse that haunts the werewolves in the present day.

We looked at each other, and I grabbed the book from him. I paced as I read, never stumbling but growing more horrified by every word.

"Once, a beautiful young dragon was encountered by a werewolf in the forest by her home. Without prior knowledge of the being, she befriended him, and the werewolf gave her every reason to believe his intentions were true. Although older than she, the werewolf decided he wanted to form a union with the dragon girl.

"He waited until she was a proper age and watched her walk around the Glistening Tree. He disguised himself as a dragon, and her parents and brothers welcomed him.

"The werewolf mated with the dragon, and an heir was produced."

I stopped, not certain if I wanted to continue. If I didn't read the rest of the story, I would be blind to the outcome, and I had a strong feeling that it was going to be terrible.

"Do you want me to finish it?" Rymon asked.

I shook my head.

"An elf had been known to visit the dragon family from time to time, and it was on one such visit that she discovered the family had been murdered. The brothers had been gutted, and the parents' eyes were ripped from their sockets. The dragon and her youngling were missing. The dragon was found a mile from her home, lying by a creek. The baby was presumed dead, as there was a pool of blood by the creek that hadn't come from the babe's mother."

I took a deep breath, willing myself to remember the tale was centuries old. I finally blinked back the tears and read on.

"The elf tore her hair in outrage and visited the local sorcerer. The family had been deceived, and it was speculated that they discovered the werewolf's true identity when the child displayed Lycan characteristics. They may have embraced him or condemned him, but at some point, the werewolf's true nature consumed him, and he destroyed the family. Seeing that love was not enough to prevent such a tragedy, the sorcerer conjured a spell that would prevent the union of a werewolf with any other species, as they were a slave to their desires and moon worship."

I snapped the book closed and threw it on the floor. "That's absolutely ridiculous!"

Rymon had been quiet, and I was surprised when he didn't mirror my outrage. I stomped my foot on the ground, but he appeared unaffected.

"Is it?" he said. "Is it so hard to believe that a werewolf did that?" He pointed to the book I had slammed down. "I believe every word of it, and I don't even think the werewolf loved her to begin with. I think he used her to get into a position where he could kill her but realized he could stalk her family, too, and be right under their noses."

"That's pathetic," I shot back. "Who do you know in our race that would harm someone?"

"Haven't you felt it?" Rymon asked, a pained expression creasing his face. "The moon's light shines mostly on the vampire's colony, but I can feel a change in me. It's like a hunger that can't be satisfied no matter how much meat I eat."

He stared at me for validation, but I couldn't help him. Maybe the moon affected him more because he had started to shift.

"I want to go into the Forbidden Zone and kill the first thing I see." His fingers looked like claws, and the points on his canines seemed sharper. "And I don't want to stop there. I want to kill the squirrels, the deer, the bears, and anything that moves." He looked almost sinister—even though his voice was calm—as birds chirped merrily outside. "I want to find a vampire and torture it." He looked at his hand as if it held the body of his enemy. "I'd drain it of every last drop of blood, and as it laid whimpering, I'd rip off its head and drive a stake through its blood-sucking heart!"

His voice rose with his last three words, and I jumped. I recovered quickly.

"Rymon, werewolves haven't been fully exposed to the full moon in decades," I said, moving carefully to the other side of him. "Understandably, you'd feel the pull of the moon, and with our bodies going crazy before the Glistening—"

"That's not it!" he snapped. "I want to kill everything!" He looked up at me, and rage burst from him.

"Do you hear me, Corryne!" he yelled. "I want to kill everything!" He moved toward me, tilting his head. "I even want to kill you."

We walked back, as silent as we were when we arrived. For once, I wished my friend would reach out to me and give me the smile I always associated with him, but he didn't try to touch me or talk to me at all.

I carried three books in my hand that I'd swiped on my way out. After Rymon's confession, I was eager to leave quickly, but I decided to explore some of the contents of the house by taking them with me.

Rymon stalked into his house and slammed the door without a backward glance. If I was unable to satisfy my blood lust, I'd probably act similarly.

I avoided my parents, as my father was telling my mother that he had been assigned to grow new crops. He was excited about the position, as it afforded him the ability to watch hybrid vegetables take shape as he tended the soil.

I shut my bedroom door softly and fell onto my belly on the bed. I read through a book with a navy blue cover, but it was mostly filled with hand-written children's stories.

Even though another book was next in the stack, I was drawn to the leather-bound copy beneath it. I shifted it out from under the book on top of it, unfastening the clasp that held it closed.

The first page was unremarkable, except for the name of the most famous wizard I knew. Archard's name had been scribbled in black ink, almost as a technicality.

I turned the page, and my breath caught in my throat.

— · —

CHAPTER 26

After I told my parents that I was going to bed early, I turned off my light and climbed out my window. I hoped Rymon wasn't watching, as my deception had nothing to do with Allistar.

I carried the book close to my chest as I ran down the streets. When I arrived at the south barrier, I sat down, crossed my legs, and laid it on my lap.

Spells swirled on the pages, and even though I wasn't a magician, I was going to try one. The book felt warmer, as if thinking about using the spells it contained gave it life.

"What are you doing?"

I jumped up so fast that the book flipped away from me. I grabbed his jacket for support, as my legs were unstable after he'd startled me.

Zaffron stared at my hand on his jacket. "I did not mean to frighten you. You aren't supposed to be here."

"I know," I said. I was struck by a thought. "Is your father making an exchange tonight?"

He appeared confused until he understood my question. "No, my father should not be here tonight. He's at home with my mother."

I let go of his jacket and made a show of straightening it. I wondered what kind of material stayed unmarred after my sharp finger-nails had dug into it.

"Why are you here then?" I asked.

He opened his mouth to answer, but nothing came out. Settling on a condescending stare, he let me reach my own conclusions. He didn't expect me to discover the truth.

"You're spying on me," I said, fully realizing it was true as I said it.

Zaffron mentioned my pride and safety, but his excuses were bogus, and I was glad to see him flustered. It entertained me. I watched him squirm and brushed imaginary dirt from his jacket, raising my eyebrows and pursing my lips.

"It's okay," I teased, pushing the issue without angering him. "It's nice to have such a *cute* protector." I smiled at him and put my hands behind his neck, pulling back to look at him.

Another misleading explanation started to tumble from his lips. "If you didn't constantly get into trouble—" He narrowed his eyes. "*Cute?* You think I'm *cute.*"

I pulled my lips in and smiled. I had wondered how long it would take him to understand my jest.

"*Cute* may be the word you use to describe the unicorn who climbs into your window, but I am not *cute.*"

"Absolutely adorable," I continued, pecking his cheek before I bent down to pick up the spell book. I didn't look up for his reaction.

"You are infuriating," he commented, but he sat beside me in the grass.

"What is that?" He pointed to the book in my hand.

I leaned in conspiratorially. "It could be the answer to our problems."

He didn't disregard my statement or seem skeptical. I opened the book, showing him the spell I intended to cast.

He stared at it thoughtfully. "That would seal the cracks in the dome?"

I nodded in response to his question. "And if this works, I'll close the dome."

At that, he seemed dubious. "That would take a lot of power. Archard was the strongest magician of his age."

"I have to try something," I told him, rubbing my temples. "And if I show the elders the book, they may not allow me to use it. Or worse, they may confiscate it and do nothing." He wasn't entirely convinced, so I added, "Or Namon could give it to his outside contacts."

His eye widened almost imperceptibly. It took him a moment to process possible outcomes, but he finally committed to helping me.

"I'll allow you to do this if you use my strength to aid with the spell."

I sighed. "You'll *allow* me to do it," I scoffed. "I'd love to see you try to stop me."

He flipped me onto my back so fast that all I saw was the darkness around me spinning. One moment, I was looking in the direction of the cracked south barrier, and the next second I was staring at a black and marginally rosy sky full of stars with Zaffron above me. He was gentle, placing one hand behind my head. With the other, he produced the spell book.

My breath came out in heavy puffs. I wasn't fearful, just surprised.

"Did I hurt you?" he asked, noticing it.

"No," I breathed, and because I wanted to continue our banter and tell him the truth without revealing that I really felt that way, I told him, "You are truly magnificent."

Zaffron startled. I expected a sarcastic response and some more wordplay, but he studied me in a way that made me feel like he was searching for deception.

I was glad the sky was mostly dark, as it was awkward to be looked at so intently. I grasped for anything I could say to dial down the intensity of his eyes. A neon fire glowed from them and then his lips were on mine, and the taste and smell of his fire consumed my thoughts.

With Rymon, I had been young, and I felt compelled to kiss him. With Allistar, he was more interested in satisfying his own desires. But with Zaffron, there seemed to be a balance. I wanted him, and he wanted me.

As we kissed, Zaffron took my hand and held it over his heart. Dragons were prideful and aggressive, but at that moment, he was open and compassionate. I put my other hand inside his shirt and traveled up his rock-hard stomach. He swatted my hand away, laughing.

"I can't let you do that," he said.

I had enjoyed his moment of unguarded mirth and sought to extend it. I struggled to put my hand back inside his shirt, but he easily moved it away. He lifted off me, turning serious.

"I do not like that."

I inched over, and it struck me that I could be as close to him as long as I didn't dance my fingers across his belly. "I've never heard you laugh," I admitted. My voice was low, and I directed it into his ear.

"I do not like it," he repeated. He sat with his knees bent and his arms draped over them.

"Okay," I smiled, even though he couldn't see it. "I'll make you a deal. I won't tickle you if you'll kiss me again."

Zaffron reached over and caressed my face, running his thumb across my cheek. It didn't take him long to bring me back to the moment we'd shared, and I found my hands roaming his back and chest, feeling every well-defined muscle.

I let his hands glide down my back, finding my hips. He squeezed them like he was going to lift me onto his lap, but he stopped himself.

"We're going too fast," he breathed out heavily.

Between our kisses and the awakened desire for each other, we had trouble catching our breaths. We were still close, and every inhale stole the exhale from the other.

He pulled away from me, assuming the same position he'd had before I asked him to kiss me. "What we're doing is not honorable. You are betrothed, and the unicorn still thinks you are his."

The change in his mood rattled me. I wanted to be with him, but he had pushed me away.

"Maybe I don't like belonging to any being," I spat.

"Then you shouldn't have pledged yourself to another," he responded curtly.

I tried to think of something that would cut him as deeply, but all I could think of is, "I didn't have a choice."

He chuckled dryly. "You always have a choice. You just have to decide if you're going to live the life others map out for you or if you're going to stop hiding like a coward."

"So, I'm a coward now?"

He sighed heavily. "You are not weak in everything you do, but your uncertainty is alarming. It's what keeps me away from you."

"Yeah," I snorted. "It looks like you're away from me."

His head shook. "It is impossible to communicate with you sometimes. You are a fledgling."

It was a low blow, especially since we were technically the same age. "I don't think I was immature when I left my house tonight to try to save the dome."

He held up his finger. "Your cause was noble, but you did not tell your parents where you were going, you were out past your curfew, and" —he pointed at the open spell book at our feet— "you are planning to endanger your life."

His eyebrows went up. "How did you get the magician's book, Corryne?"

I answered him before I thought it through, my impulsiveness awakened by our argument. "I found it at his house."

His head snapped in my direction. "You found Archard's home?"

I realized my mistake, and I tried to cover it. Zaffron dismissed all my excuses and pressed me for the truth. After I failed to mislead him, I told him about the hidden road next to the fairies' neighborhood and the items Rymon and I had liberated.

"That is a stolen book," Zaffron observed. "That will affect its magic."

I rolled my eyes. "Would it make you feel better if I put it back after I tried the spell?"

"No," he replied. "It would make me feel better if you hadn't taken it at all."

I reached for the book, and I flipped to the page I had marked. "Well, it's here, so I'm going to do what I can to save our home."

Zaffron didn't make a move to stop me, so I assumed that I had won the point. Due to my nature, my eyes adjusted to the dark well, and the script was easy for me to read.

The spell was laced with words from another language, but it sounded like gibberish when I spoke it. At one point, the wind around us blew harder, making it difficult to read the words. As I neared the end, the text began to swirl, and when my cadence faltered, Zaffron took my hand in his own.

The hazy red light in the dome seemed to flicker, almost like we were in a horror movie. Zaffron continued to hold onto me, and I thought I felt sparks of power move from him into me, but that could have been my imagination. The words to the spell ended, and I sat there wondering if I needed to repeat it or if it only required uttering one time.

Zaffron suggested that we explore the crack, and he lifted me to my feet. I was a little wobbly at first, but he steadied me, and I walked to the barrier. I ran my hand along the fissure, but there was no air filtering through it. Instead, a gooey substance sealed it and hardened under my touch.

Without thinking of our previous argument, I turned and embraced Zaffron. "I did it!" I cried happily.

"You did it," he echoed with less excitement.

He touched the product of my spell and nodded. "What are you going to do when my father finds out that his place of exchange is sealed?"

"He won't know it was me," I said. "He'd probably begin looking at the elders first."

Zaffron scoffed. "The elders are complacent. The spell reeks of a new, inexperienced being."

It was the second time I felt like he'd attacked my abilities. Anger stirred in my chest.

"You know, if I'm so inexperienced, then why do you seem to like me so much?"

He stood still in the darkness, not speaking.

"You talk about the way I act with you when I'm betrothed and might or might not have a boyfriend, but it didn't stop you from kissing me."

"You're impulsive," he noted. "You speak rashly."

"And you talk like a haughty old man!" I shouted at him. Our disagreement was starting to take a toll on me, and I had to blink to shift my eyes into focus. "Do you think kissing me was a well-planned strategy of some kind?"

He straightened, and the sides of his mouth tugged up before he resisted their upward movement. "That's easily debatable."

"Uh!" I yelled out in frustration, and a nearby dog barked its disapproval. "What was I thinking?" I paced away from him but turned around and pointed at him. "I'll tell you what I was thinking. I thought every time you kissed me or touched me it felt right. When you held my hand over your heart, I wanted to be in it. I wanted to be your every thought." I stopped before I said everything on my mind.

Zaffron looked at the ground. He opened his mouth to speak, but he closed it quickly.

I thought I knew what he was going to say. "I know, you're a dragon."

It was so much more than a statement of the obvious. As a dragon, Zaffron was expected to breed with his own kind. There was no future for us, and the more I thought about it, the less I wanted to be with him.

I stalked off in the other direction, and he called after me. He caught up quickly, even though I should have been much faster than him on the ground.

"Corryne," he implored. "We should talk. I—"

I was tired of talking, and my mind was set on another task. I tripped over an indention in the ground, and he caught me before I fell. I continued to march away from him until he called my name.

Within seconds he was beside me. "What are you doing?"

I turned around with my hands on my hips. "I'm going to close the top of the dome."

For the first time, an emotion-like concern passed across his features. "I don't think it's wise to do that tonight."

"Well, it's a good thing you aren't in charge, isn't it?"

Zaffron stood at his full height, almost a foot taller than me. "I do not claim to own you, but you should listen to my advice. Dragons are revered for their wisdom."

I snorted. "Not seventeen-year-old dragons."

I thought he rolled his eyes, but it was dark, so I couldn't be certain. "Please wait until tomorrow to seal the uppermost part of the dome. You are weakened by your experience at the southern point, and I'm afraid you will hurt yourself."

A combination of irritation and flattery hit me at once. It was Zaffron's soft tone that skewed me over to flattery, and I gave in.

"Fine. I won't close the dome tonight, but are there any other cracks I can seal?"

Zaffron was silent for so long that I thought he wasn't going to answer me. He finally spoke with hesitation. "I know a place, but it's several miles away." He extended his hand. "Do you trust me?"

I took his hand without another thought. "Yes." As I replied, I realized it was true. I trusted Zaffron, even though he was infuriating, and his father could be a traitor.

Zaffron pulled me to him, and we embraced awkwardly, as he had to spread his wings. I felt weightless as he lifted vertically, but then I was ultra-aware of my weight and the air around me when Zaffron settled into a horizontal path, flapping his wings once for every five beats of my hammering heart.

Zaffron held me firmly, but his arms weren't restrictive. If I had been able to fly, he would have allowed me to loosen my grip when I was ready, but he seemed content to hold onto me, too. Zaffron was more at home in the sky than he was on the ground, and his spirit was lighter. When he noticed me looking at him, he kissed my forehead. It was a chaste kiss, and I lifted my head, hopeful that he would kiss me as we flew, but he looked away, staring purposefully away. Finally, he touched down and placed my feet on the grass.

"We're here," he announced.

I could walk, but I allowed him to guide me to the place.

"The flashing light from the last spell should have alerted the vampires, but this will be the last area they will check," Zaffron told me. "Just hurry."

I set to work immediately, placing the book on my lap as Zaffron joined me on the grass. He held my hand, and when I glanced at him, he nodded.

Zaffron had flown us to a crack, and it appeared much larger than the one on the south end. It was open at the very base of the dome, and I imagined I could squeeze through it. I entertained the idea of sneaking out of the dome and running into a world that had always been just beyond my reach.

I wanted to repeat my thoughts to Zaffron, but I knew he'd tell me I was being selfish by placing myself and the other beings in the dome at risk. After all, if I could get out, what was to stop a small elf from breaching our border and slowly assassinating our leaders?

I started speaking the words of the spell, and a wind from an unknown source lifted my hair. I didn't chance a look at Zaffron, but he seemed to be consumed, too, as bits of his raven hair flipped into my vision.

Just as before, the light in the dome flickered, but this time, a grumbling escaped the earth as the glass began to shift. Voices shouted through the night, breaking my concentration, and ending the spell.

I saw Allistar first, and my heart did a double skip. Maybe he had seen me with Zaffron, and he was jealous, or better yet, maybe he wanted to help us seal the crack. With Allistar's blooming magic, we could close the dome immediately.

Then I saw her.

I knew it was Mariam, even though she stayed mostly in the shadows. Whether Allistar had told her to, or she was afraid of us, she tried to stay hidden, but she didn't understand that supernaturals can sense humans without the use of sight. I could smell her fruity perfume and the honey in her hair.

I couldn't speak. For once, I was glad Zaffron did it for me.

"You brought a human into the dome?" he yelled at Allistar. "How could you endanger us all?"

Allistar ran a hand down his silvery hair, and the way it reflected in the moonlight made my mouth water. It was a strange reaction at an inopportune moment, but as soon as I felt the urge it was gone, making me wonder if I had felt it at all.

"It's fine!" Allistar yelled back at him. "Nothing's happened because of it."

Zaffron gestured to the dome around us. "Hasn't it? Maybe your secret is the reason our protection is failing us."

Mariam darted from her hiding place to the open crack. Without a backward glance, she slipped through. Although it had seemed difficult for her to squeeze through, she had made it quickly to the other side. Once she was free of the dome, she ran into the night, and I lost sight of her almost immediately.

"Your cowardly human ran away," I observed.

Both boys turned to me.

"Don't talk about her like that!" Allistar yelled at me. "At least she knows what she wants and she's willing to give her heart over completely."

I laughed dryly. "So, she has sex with you. I'm sorry to tell you, that's not her heart. And the way you chase after me doesn't show that you love her either."

"Maybe I wouldn't have been with Mariam if you had told everyone we were together," he shot back. "I didn't like being your secret."

"Whatever!" I spat. "Bredek told us you were with her before you ever kissed me."

He crossed his arms and smiled smugly. "Then it sounds like this is your fault."

I was struck speechless. *How were his cheating and deception my fault?* Before I could sling back a retort, a voice boomed in our direction.

"What are you kids doing here?"

Allistar was the farthest away, and he darted into the shadows, disappearing from view. A spotlight shone on Zaffron and me. Zaffron stepped in front of me, blocking the light from my eyes.

"You can follow the unicorn," he whispered.

I wasn't going to run off with my tail tucked between my legs. Allistar may have been happy to save his skin, but I wasn't going to leave Zaffron to take the punishment. I put my hand on his back.

I was strong in my resolve until a familiar figure stepped out and recognized me. I held my head high as the griffins approached us with handcuffs.

"Hold on right there," my brother called out, almost laughing. "This one" —he pointed at me— "is underage. I don't know about the other one."

"We are in the same year," I spoke quickly. I thought I was saving Zaffron from a trip to the holding facility, but he didn't seem pleased with my effort. His face hardened.

My brother stared at me like he had been awarded the raise he always complained wasn't given to him. "Well, well, well. What will Mom and Dad have to say about this?"

—·—

Chapter 27

Hamlet was unmerciful. He placed Zaffron and me in separate cars, asking a griffin to take Zaffron to his father's dwelling while he took me home.

The griffin, Azarra, spoke to me kindly, reminding me that everyone had been out after their curfew at one time or another, and softening the effect my brother's presence was having on me. She put her hand on my arm as Hamlet discussed some of my history with another griffin. My past was unflattering, and it was hard to hear my brother dredge up my mistakes.

Most griffins' feathers were yellow and orange, but Azarra had purple, green, and blue. Far from flaunting her naturally symmetrical beauty and colorful feathers, she wore no makeup and held her feathers tightly to her skin.

Once, when Hamlet let out a laugh over the irony of assisting the team who caught me, Azarra said, "We've all made mistakes, and we can only grow and learn by making more."

Hamlet seemed deeply affected by Azzara's statement. He continued with his work without haughty insults or spontaneous laughter over my misfortune.

Zaffron and I were separated, but I could see him speaking proudly to Azarra when she asked him questions. I didn't know what he was saying to her, so I opted to tell the truth and leave out the part about Archard's spell book. Once the cruisers' doors were closed, I tried to get Zaffron's attention, but he stared straight ahead.

I couldn't imagine what he was going to face. It was likely that Namon would close him in a cave for a number of years until the memory of his actions was forgotten. I'd heard about dragon parents who preferred that type of punishment, and Namon's pride was strong. I hoped Zaffron's mother was too endeared to her son to part with him in such a way.

My brother locked me in the backseat of his cruiser and ran back to where they had found us. I didn't look behind me. When he returned, he chatted happily as he drove.

"I told them it was a waste of their time to keep you in the house after they caught you with the unicorn." He was referring to conversations he'd had with our parents. It stung deeply when I thought about my mother and father revealing their horror over my mistake as they spoke to my brother.

He made a gagging sound. "Really? A unicorn. How could you even get past their smell?"

I wanted to get back at him, but all I had were words. "He smelled like strawberries, and I love strawberries."

"I eat strawberries," he responded without humor. "I don't sleep with them."

I had a strong feeling that he thought I had given over myself to Allistar and then to Zaffron. I had drifted from one to the other, but I had only kissed them. I opened my mouth to tell him so, but then I closed it. I honestly didn't care what he thought of me.

The miles passed quickly, and my house came into view. My stomach flopped when I saw my mom was already waiting on the porch. The light behind her made her a dark shadow in front of my house.

Hamlet laughed and glanced back at me. "I may have made a phone call before the drive over."

I thought there would be yelling and fighting. I thought I would be restricted to my room until Glistening Day. Instead, when Hamlet and I walked to the steps my mother placed a suitcase and a duffle bag at my feet.

She turned on her heel and walked into the house. Her meaning was resolute and final. The door closed securely behind her, and I vowed never to cross the threshold again.

"I guess *you're* happy!" I barked at Hamlet.

He appeared stunned, and it was a moment before he registered my voice. He shook his head, and a concerned look crossed his features.

"No, Corryne. I didn't expect that."

I threw my hands up. "What did you think would happen?"

He narrowed his eyes. "You're the perfect offspring. I didn't think they'd toss you out."

I picked up the suitcase and slung the duffle bag over my shoulder. "Yeah, sure. You thought our mother would stand for her daughter to be a two-time blood traitor."

"So, you are involved with the dragon's spawn."

I sighed and shook my head. "We're just friends. I mean, I've kissed him, but we know our places."

"You're lucky then."

I was shocked. All my life, I'd seen him as borderline cruel and depressed but perfectly comfortable in his werewolf skin.

Realization struck me. "The griffin. The one who took Zaffron home. You're involved with Azarra."

He growled and stalked back to his cruiser. "I have *never* crossed that line."

Suddenly, I was full of pity for my brother. "But she seemed so nice, and she doesn't look like she'd mind it if you asked her to unite."

He glared at me. "You're too young to understand our differences." He pointed to the car. "Are you getting in, or do you want to walk to your boyfriend's house?"

I didn't want to show up on Zaffron's doorstep, and I told him so. I suggested Fiona's house.

"I don't know if the faeries will like what you've done any better," he said seriously. "They're pretty loyal creatures, and you broke your promise to Rymon twice."

"Only once," I countered. "I never confirmed my acceptance of his proposal until two weeks ago."

"Then why did you shave him?" Hamlet asked. "I think that was confirmation enough."

I put my head in my hands. "Poor Rymon. He really didn't deserve this."

Hamlet agreed. "You could have told him from the beginning that you weren't interested in him."

"I tried!" I cried.

"How hard did you try?"

I shook my head. "He wouldn't listen. He kept thinking I'd warm to him."

"You had better options than me."

I couldn't see it from his angle but softened my tone. "You still have options."

"Maybe," he conceded. "If I want to break my mother's heart and have my father disown me, too."

It was harsh to hear it that way. The word *disown* sank into my skin like a brand.

We pulled up in front of Fiona's house, and he stopped the car. His posture drooped, and he stared at the steering wheel.

"I think it's understood that we're through here."

I felt like cold water had been thrown on my face.

Hamlet went on. "I don't want to see you or talk to you again. And after you walk under the Glistening Tree, I won't hesitate to arrest you if you've disobeyed the law. That includes intermarrying."

I didn't owe him anything. His only kindness to me had been the short drive to my friend's house.

As I stepped out of the cruiser, he added, "I hope you find what you're looking for."

I closed the door on him and everyone with similar beliefs. I was finished living under the rules of the dome. I was either going to change them or tear down the dome myself.

I could have tapped at my friends' bedroom window, but I decided to be honest, or as honest as possible. I knocked at the door and shielded my eyes when the porch light turned on.

My friends' father answered the door, rubbing his green eyes. His spiky blond hair was too short to appear disheveled, but his blue and white pajama suit was rumpled.

"What are you doing here, Corryne?"

I pointed to my luggage. "My parents kicked me out. Can I stay here for the rest of the night?"

His face sobered. "If your parents kicked you out, that's grounds for banishment. I can't be part of that."

"Davis," a voice cooed. "It's just for one night, and the night is half over."

My friends' mother appeared, wrapping her olive-toned arms around her husband's waist. "Besides, Corryne has always been good, and you know how strict the wolves can be."

She pouted her full lips, and Davis caved, allowing me entry. I put my duffle bag and suitcase by the couch, and Davis returned to his room, scratching his neck.

She walked down the hall and returned with bedsheets and a pillow as bright as the sun's light.

After Davis's first wife had died in childbirth, he married Lilith. She was long-limbed with eyes like dark pools and long ebony hair. It was easy to see my friends looked more like their mother.

"Now, don't worry about my husband," Lilith told me, fluffing my pillow. "You sleep as long as you want and eat breakfast with us in the morning."

I expressed my appreciation, and she surprised me by hugging me. She rocked, and I moved with the motion.

"Do you want to talk about it?" she asked.

I entertained telling Lilith about my experience and conflicted feelings, but I held back. What if she didn't want to help me anymore after she found out about my close call with the police?

"Not right now."

She gave me another gentle squeeze around my shoulders. "I understand, precious girl. It's still too fresh."

Lilith had a voice almost like a song, and every time she spoke, she could make everyday phrases seem like melodies. Aside from the ones in my year, I didn't have a lot of experience with fayries, so the trait may have been common. I was always a little entranced, and sometimes unnerved, by the feeling of peacefulness Lilith could transmit with her voice.

I tried to sleep, but every time I had a dream, I woke myself up. I thought about Zaffron in a dark cave, wasting away under his father's watchful eyes. I dreamed about loving moments with my parents, sharing a board game, or walking hand-in-hand. Just as the sun peeked over the mountains, my eyes flew open, and a new anxiety took shape.

I had been so concerned with Zaffron and then with my situation that my mind hadn't registered Archard's spell book. I scanned my mind, and as I relived the scene, I confirmed that the book wasn't on the ground where I'd dropped it.

Archard's spell book was gone.

—·—

CHAPTER 28

"What happened?" Fallyn whispered.

They didn't need to talk in low voices, as I had been awake for over an hour. Lilith stirred something in a bowl, stopping to answer her daughter.

"Her parents disowned her. Your father and I let her stay here last night."

"Are they going to have her banished?" Fallyn gasped.

"Who's getting banished?" Fiona asked as she entered the room. Her voice echoed in the otherwise muted morning.

"Shh!" Fallyn and Lilith told her simultaneously.

I imagined my friend's startled face.

"What?"

Hushed whispers followed her question, and the trio shared their feelings on a frequency they thought I couldn't hear. As a werewolf, though, once I tuned in to sounds, I could hear everything.

"Maureen has already requested an emergency meeting with the council," Lilith divulged.

"What was so bad that they granted her request?" Fiona wondered. "There are way bigger problems than a teenager sneaking out."

"She was with a dragon."

"Which one?" Notes of conspiracy hung in her voice. "Was it one of the older—?"

"It was Zaffron," Fiona answered her plainly. The women must have exchanged a glace, because Fiona added, "He stares at her all the time. He's done it for years."

My heartbeat quickened, drowning out the sound of their chatter for a moment. *Zaffron had liked me for years? Why hadn't I noticed it before?*

"What are they going to do to him?" Fiona asked. "Surely he will have the same punishment."

"His punishment will be worse," Lilith replied. "Namon may restrict him to the caves until your generation of beings dies out."

"Would he do that to his own son?" Fallyn inquired, her voice quivering. Restriction to the caves meant solitude, and faeries never spent a moment alone.

"Of course he would," Fiona spat.

"Calida will not allow it," Lilith interjected. "She loves her son more than all the jewels in her home."

It was past time for me to announce my consciousness, so I let out a loud yawn. Immediately, the sounds of stirring and other busy movements drifted to me. Satisfied that the women were unaware I'd heard them, I entered the kitchen and offered to help prepare breakfast.

"I have it, my dear," Lilith chirped, whipping pancake batter with blueberries the size of my thumb. Some of them popped, turning the mixture a dark purple.

Davis didn't appear until the pancakes were placed on the table. I waited as the family took their seats, and Lilith pointed to a seat beside her. I joined them, and they insisted that I eat first. I took one pancake, but Lilith encouraged me to take four. She could have thought it would be my last meal before I was banished.

After we'd eaten, Davis wiped his mouth with a cloth napkin and put his hands on the table. He seemed unhappy about the news he had to deliver.

"There's something unpleasant we must discuss."

"Am I banished?" It popped out of my mouth before I could stop myself.

He wouldn't look at me. "That depends on what the council decides."

Fiona popped out of her seat. "But you're on the council, Dad. Can't you do something?"

Davis stood, facing her fully and firmly. "Yes, I have a position on the council, but mine is only one voice." He pointed at me. "She has a history of cavorting with other species', so it will be hard to get the council to understand, especially Namon, Lycon, Sitali, and Ledot."

"Lycon won't banish me."

Davis forced a laugh. "I wouldn't be so sure. He doesn't vote for anything unless it promotes the protection of the dome."

I thought back to my interactions with Lycon. It was true that he had been upset when I mentioned fighting, but that was because he was in favor of running away. I didn't want to argue with my friends' father, though, so I kept my opinion tucked behind my lips.

Davis and Fiona sat down, and Lilith popped up to clear the plates. I tried to help, but she waved away my efforts.

Fallyn took my hand and led me to her room. She turned on some music, and a pop star compared her tee shirts with another girl's skirts.

"As far as I'm concerned, you're a faerie," Fallyn declared. She noticed my horrified face and added, "You know, like my family adopted you." Fiona nodded along from her bed.

Fallyn and Fiona had a brightly lit room that seemed to reflect every ray of the early morning sun. Fallyn's side of the room was decorated in orange tones, like the sunset, from her bedspread to the frames of her ballerina pictures. Fiona's bedspread was yellow, like the breaking dawn, and even her desk had tones of lemon and honey on the handles and drawers.

Fallyn handed me a butterscotch sundress. It was beautiful, and I admired the delicate details, but I shook my head.

"You know I'm a werewolf, right?"

She rolled her eyes. "Of course I know what you are. I mean, you wear these bulky black pants" —she pointed to them— "and plain white or black shirts all the time." She sighed deeply. "But you're planning to throw yourself on the mercy of the council, and this dress will make you look sweet and innocent."

"Or completely ridiculous," I jabbed.

"Hey! That's my dress!" Fiona exclaimed, and I had a brief memory of her in it.

I closed my eyes. When I opened them, I decided to accept my friends' help and guidance.

"I'm sorry, Fiona. The dress is beautiful."

Fiona gave me a half-smile. "Fallyn's not wrong, you know. You should consider wearing the dress."

Fallyn dragged me to her bathroom and pointed to each one of the bottles in their shower caddy and the ones on their bathroom counter, lined up like medicines at an apothecary. I tried to pay attention, but there was an array of beauty products I didn't even know existed.

Faerie's lived long lives, and they aged slowly, so even though Davis and Lilith looked like they were middle-aged, they could have lived one hundred years or more. It was the same for unicorns, dragons, and mermaids. Werewolves and griffins had similar lifespans, and druids died as quickly—and almost as easily—as humans. Vampires and elves seemed to possess immortality, although, I had my doubts about it.

With their preserved beauty and longevity, I didn't think faeries needed so many products, but they used the herbs and other plants from their thriving gardens to make everything they put into and onto their bodies. At one time, I had seen their preoccupation as vanity, but over the years, I understood it was a highly industrious process.

She tossed two round disks into the shower. When my eyebrows rose, she explained, "They're shower enhancers. Those" —she pointed to them— "are lavender. Lavender is calming, and you need it."

I didn't think I appeared overly stressed, but I had a tiring day ahead. I accepted her idea. After all, if I were banished, I'd be bathing in the creeks.

Once Fallyn left me, I undressed and stepped into their stone shower. Two sprays of water hit me from different directions and caused a fine mist to drift up to my eyes. I blinked away the extra water and peered over my choices in the shower caddy.

All I needed was shampoo and soap, and I found a shampoo with a dandelion suspended inside the bottle. The contents of the bottle were thick, and a small amount washed my hair. Realizing Fallyn would call me out if I didn't use it, I put dandelion conditioner on my ends. I washed with a honey-based body wash and wondered if the bees would attack me when I stepped outside, as it was so powerful that it masked the lavender permeating the air.

Fallyn and Fiona fussed over my hair and makeup until they deemed me acceptable. When I looked in the mirror, I could hardly recognize myself, and if it weren't for my pointy canines, I could have passed for a faerie.

Davis and Lilith were equally shocked by my new look. They shared a glance before complimenting me.

I inclined my head to Fallyn and then Fiona. "It was their idea. They wanted me to look innocent."

Davis pinched his chin between his thumb and forefinger. "That's not a bad idea."

"Are we ready to go?" Fiona asked.

Davis shook his head. "Oh no, young lady. You will not be going with us to the council meeting."

"Why not?" Fallyn and Fiona said in unison.

"Because it's a closed session," Lilith responded firmly. "The two of you will go to school."

"What?" Fiona cried. "And what if they banish Corryne before we get home?"

"Then you should say your goodbyes now," Davis replied.

Even to me, it was a little harsh, but I knew he was right. My friends wouldn't be allowed inside the hearing, and if I were banished, I'd be led out of the doors by vampires, so it was better for them to go to school.

They embraced me, but we weren't allowed to shed tears as we rushed through our farewells. Fallyn tried to give me a pendant, and Fiona ran to the kitchen to prepare more food, but their parents stopped them. Once banished, you were stripped of everything you owned, only wearing a council-provided smock when led to the barrier.

My friends left for class, and Lilith packed our lunches. "We'll likely be there most of the day," she said. "Why don't you grab a book from the library in case you need it to pass the time?"

I followed her advice, but the books in their library were about war or faeries. I wondered just what my mother had packed for me when she'd disowned me, and I decided to investigate my luggage.

In the suitcase, I found nothing but clothes, but in the duffle bag, my mother had packed books, my diary, and pictures. Apparently, she had ripped the photographs with me in them from the walls, as some of them were from my younger years and others had cracked frames. Rymon had talked us into a couple of family photos, and she had included all of them. It seemed I had been erased from their lives completely.

Lilith walked in as I was holding our last family photo. In it, my mother and brother wore matching thin-lipped smiles, and my father stared up at the camera with wide-eyed shock. Rymon had snapped the picture quickly as I was laughing over something he had said.

Lilith placed her delicate hand on my shoulder. "Are you ready to go, sweet girl?"

I nodded. I pushed the picture back into the duffle bag and grabbed one of the books without looking at it.

I blinked away my tears and stood at my full height. I was ready to face the council and the people who had once called me their daughter.

— • —

CHAPTER 29

The council convened in a small courtroom. The larger courtroom was reserved for adult matters, and as I had not passed under the Glistening Tree, I was considered a minor.

The courthouse was a two-story beige brick structure with four columns and a metal roof. The building was airy, but the rooms downstairs were compact. Upstairs, there was one large courtroom and a smaller room that was used for juveniles.

When we entered, we waited in a queue for an identification badge. Davis didn't need one, as he was a council member, but he stood with Lilith and me.

The receptionist was one of Davis's and Lilith's sons. He had graduated in Hamlet's year, and I thought his name was Devin. He was kind to me, but he cringed when he heard the reason I was visiting the building.

The fayrie I assumed was Devin gave visitor passes to Lilith and me. Davis led us up two flights of narrow steps, and a vampire patted Davis down. Guns had been limited under the dome, but beings were still careful, as tensions sometimes ran high. The vampire hardly touched Lilith and didn't bother to check me. I didn't know the reason until he spoke.

"I can smell the fear on you, young one. You don't need a weapon; you need a miracle."

The council didn't see us right away.

Davis left Lilith and me on a padded wooden bench as he joined them. The building was so quiet that I could hear his feet as he strode down the hall, but I couldn't make out the conversations behind closed doors.

Lilith opened the basket she'd carried inside with our lunches and produced our books. She handed my selection to me, and it was then that I noticed the book I had chosen. No title adorned the cover, and the pages were handwritten. There seemed to have been several pages that had been ripped out from the front, and the writing read like a journal, even though there were no dates, only two spaces between each entry. The script was plain and easy to read, so I started at the beginning.

I had the dream again.

I was underwater, watching the mermaids in their capital city. The only indication I had that this was the city of Marilla was the brilliantly constructed shell castle. Children played, swimming after each other happily as parents watched over them with endearing smiles.

The water darkened, and the castle shook, small pieces crumbling from the sides. I tried to step away, but I was a silent observer, trapped in my own disembodied state.

A merman rose from the debris, but as he regained his composure, his challenger, another merman with purple highlights in his dark hair and a robust, muscular frame, bore down upon him, spearing him with a mighty trident. Thankfully, I was not forced to witness the outcome of their battle, but I was certain of the victor.

I was pulled to the shore by an invisible force, and I looked on as the merman brought his bloody trident to the shore. Elves and druids flocked to him, and he marched them away with orders. The screams I heard came from almost every being, males, females, and their young offspring. Even the ones who fought bravely met a swift doom, as an elf's skill is unmatched. Almost all the magical creatures were unmercifully slaughtered.

As he watched the genocide of innocents, the usurper lay across his throne with an unwilling court of mermaids. Three sisters and their mother sat in chains at his feet. The youngest met my eyes. She was the most like me in her extra-sensory abilities.

"Kill him," she begged me.

I shook my head, knowing only a shift in my vision was an indication that I had moved it. There are many things I have done, both great and horrible, but I have never taken a life.

The young mermaid visibly slumped. She stared at the hard surfaces around her and back at me. "If you will not kill him, then you must trap him. If you don't seal him in the sea, he will destroy everything."

I nodded. "I will do as you ask."

She looked over at the older girls, and I assumed they were her sisters. "Please try to save us. But if you can't, let him kill us."

I must have gasped because Lilith put her hand on my knee. I looked up at her with a blank stare, still back in the world of mermen and death.

"A book can be a good distraction," she commented.

I nodded my head automatically, but my mind was still miles away. It was obvious that I had swiped Archard's journal when I had grabbed the books at his home. I wondered what else I'd find on the pages. I read the next entry.

Her blue-green eyes haunt me.

She's the usurper's daughter, the sister of the young mermaid who asked for my help. I can't understand why she's so important when her sisters' outwardly talents are so obvious. Does she have a power that hides just below the surface?

When Kano killed his brother, Davis was out of control. His dark magic swirled just behind his eyes, and I knew it was only a matter of time before he lashed out with his own plans, so I gave him a task.

I told him to find the young mermaid that plagued my dreams, but he did even more. He sent me reports of the family and centered his focus on a girl in his year, Cascade, who didn't seem to possess talents but was clearly Kano's offspring. He wavered between asking me to get closer to her and killing her in her sleep. How can I keep him on this mission and place the young lady in harm's way?

It's unclear to me if the young girl, who I now know is Nixie, is Kano's daughter. She did not divulge that information to me in my dreams/visions, either because she's ashamed of her origins or it's untrue. There are several ways a seer can be born, and her parentage works either way.

I finally offered Davis an alternative. I packaged some malroot and sent it through Cyprus, my most trusted confidant. I told him it would poison the sisters against the sea and win them over in our favor. I wrote to him, and in the letter, I did not mention the length of time malroot would be effective. I have observed its potency over three days, but no longer. Davis, however, will expect its results to be permanent.

It seemed to work. Now, I must wait as he devises a plan to give each of the sisters the malroot. It may take some time, but I am a patient man.

I had suspected Davis was older than my parents, and Archard's journal had confirmed it. It seemed Davis had been a vengeful faerie, and I didn't know him well enough to determine if he'd accepted his brother's death or if he held hatred for King Kano. Even though the faeries were full of light, he might have taken a life, darkening his heart forever.

I glanced over at Lilith, who was reading a small brown book with golden-edged pages. A simple smile graced her lips. *Did she know she was married to a monster?*

Fallyn, Fiona, and I had been friends since we started classes, and I had known Davis since he picked them up on the first day of school. Unlike most faeries, he wasn't as affectionate with his daughters, but as a werewolf, I had dismissed it. Lilith was the embodiment of a faerie, with her kindness and compassion, yet Davis was only nice and casually indifferent on his best days, though. Now, I knew some of the reasons for it.

Davis had been Archard's soldier. And, I surmised, he was a sociopath.

I felt a little differently about the course of the trial. I thought Davis would vote in my favor, but if he sought revenge against innocents at such a young age, he was capable of anything.

It seemed Davis had conflicting feelings about Cascade. *Had he acted on them, or had he poisoned her and her sisters, bringing them to the dome as slaves?* The latter seemed unlikely, as I'd never seen a mermaid under the dome.

A memory of the lake in the Forbidden Zone surfaced, but I quickly dismissed it. Mermaids were territorial creatures. If one had caught me, it wouldn't have let me go.

That meant Davis had either killed the family or had allowed them to be captured by King Kano. Both possibilities seemed cruel.

Lilith handed me a sandwich and nodded to me to continue reading. She must have misread my preoccupation, assuming my interest in the book outweighed my fear of the upcoming hearing.

I chewed the honeyed bread and savored the taste of the garden vegetables. I craved meat, but faeries made their plant-based cheese from cashews, and the protein from it must have been enough to sustain me.

I flipped through several entries that spoke about disagreements he'd had with his sister, Amalthea, and the plans Archard had made for her future. Archard had assumed the role of her parent, and she seemed to rebel against him in small ways, like spying on him as he tried difficult spells and sneaking out late at night.

I scanned through most of those pages, as their family drama had nothing to do with my life under the dome Archard had created. I had almost given up when the tone of the entries changed.

I don't want them to rely on me.

They've gathered outside my home, expecting a miracle, but I can't give them everything they want. With the help of Amalthea and Cyprus, I have constructed the blueprint required for the spell.

The dome is beautiful! It encapsulates our sweet small town and makes it a haven for the remaining mythical creatures. Soon, I will cast the spell that will push the humans from their homes. It's unfortunate for them to relocate with only the items they can store in their vehicles, but it's better for them than becoming trapped with vampires and were-wolves.

I formulated a brief outline for the structure of society once we are cut off from the rest of humanity and supernaturals. I fear for the future harmony of our generations, but the mythical creatures who form our system will still feel the effects of Kano's tyranny, so they will govern with more compassion and unity.

I laughed dryly, and Lilith looked up from her book. She returned to it when I continued to read.

I'm tired, and I'm concerned that I won't have enough power to complete the spell. It's difficult to maintain an invisible barrier around my home and body, but I must keep us safe.

Amalthea doesn't understand. She thinks the energy I use to maintain our home's cooking and cleaning is minimal, and normally, she'd be correct, but now that I must watch the horizon for intruders with my mind's eye, every ounce of my power is needed.

Not only could she help with the meals and dusting, but Amalthea should stop sneaking out at night. I haven't been able to scry her position, as her defenses are strong, but it keeps me up pacing the floor at all hours until she returns. If I told her I was aware of her nightly excursions, they would continue, possibly extending past the early morning hours.

I wondered where Amalthea was going. *Did she have a secret lover?* She seemed to support her brother's idea of a dome, so staging a resistance against him was unlikely. That only left my theory of a lover. But *if she was interested in a being, who was it?*

I heard the approach of footsteps, and I waited for my name to be called. The footstep continued, though, and Nava appeared. She met another troll at the stairs, and he handed her a stack of food in closed containers. She accepted it gratefully, casting a benign smile in our direction as she passed us. Low murmuring escaped the room as Nava opened the door, but it was silenced quickly when the door closed.

I thought about discussing the journal with Lilith, but I decided against it. I couldn't refuse her if she asked to see the book, and if she thumbed through it, she might find her husband's name. I decided to finish the journal entry and make polite conversation until my hearing.

Davis hasn't contacted me in several months, and I fear the worst. It's my fault if the family has been murdered. I thought if I gave him a purpose it would steer him away from his grief.

My poor cousin! I can't imagine how it must have felt to lose his brother! Without my sister, I'd be lost, and I don't know what I'd do to the person responsible for her untimely death. Most likely, I would do nothing. Nothing is certain, though, until it is suffered.

I reached out to a dragon, Arcane, who attends the same school as Davis and Cascade. He seemed indifferent to my attempts to employ him with gems and gold, but he responded to my offer to live under the dome. He insisted that he was bringing six other beings in addition to himself, and I agreed. Seven more supernaturals shouldn't tip the scales.

While I wait for Arcane's report, I will gather the supplies we need. The faeries have offered their most precious seeds for food, and the trolls have herded their cattle and forest animals into the land for the beings who consume meat and blood. It seems I am bringing the animals here for breeding and slaughter, but I can't deny nourishment to the beings who have asked for my help.

I can only hope there will be a balance. If not, in the years after we perish, may a seer slip through a crack in the ancient structure I plan to create and dismantle it. All they have to do is destroy the source of its power.

"Corryne of Tribe Werewolf." The voice was cold and made my skin crawl, marking its owner unmistakably. When we followed her down the hall, I wasn't surprised that the council had sent Ledot to collect me. Vampires and werewolves had a history of tensions, and I wasn't immune to Ledot's withering stares.

She opened the door to the small room, and the voices hushed. All nine council members were present, as Ledot shared the position with her mother Sitali.

I took my place at a podium with a long microphone protruding from the top. Lilith stood beside me.

My mother and father entered through another door with their backs turned to me. I didn't expect them to look at me, but I had hoped my father would be less resolved. He seemed just as determined as my mother, though, holding her hand and avoiding my gaze.

Davis and the other tribe leaders sat in a line facing us. A cherry desk sat in front of each of them, with microphones snaking out of the top of each.

Davis banged a gavel and announced: "We are convening today to discuss the emergency banishment of Corryne of Tribe Werewolf."

CHAPTER 30

It was hard for me to hear the accounts of my behavior from my mother's perspective. She was the spokesperson for my parents, and I was happy about it, as it prevented my father from saying anything negative about me. Unfortunately, his stance was clear when I saw his head bobbing along with my mother's points.

With each accusal, the council listened. Their eyes were fixed on my mother, but I couldn't tell if she'd won their favor. Even Lycon's face was a mask as he paused to scribble something on a notepad in front of him before lifting his eyes again.

Sometime during my mother's rant over my behavior, Lilith took my hand in hers. I accepted the gesture, and Davis stared hard at us from his seat.

"The dome is suffering because of decisions like hers," my mother concluded. "We can see it as the dome cracks all around us. Corryne has become a blood traitor twice in the period of some months, and I fear that if her behavior is left unchecked, other offspring her age might follow her example. I feel that the council has no other choice but to banish her."

She had refrained from calling me her daughter through her address, and she didn't acknowledge my presence in the room. It was a common practice with beings who had disowned their young. It happened most frequently with werewolves, so I had seen it first-hand. Sons and daughters had cried for their parents, only to be met with closed lips and stiff backs.

Namon's attention had wavered at the end of her speech, and he had been lazily pushing around a pencil, but at my mother's closing remark, his eye shot up. "The council will make the decision *we* feel is best."

My mother nodded and took her seat, chastised.

Davis seemed unwilling to take the lead over any part of the proceedings as his wife held my hand. Lycon seemed equally conflicted since he had a personal connection to my parents and me. Sensing their reluctance, Aella moved the meeting forward.

"Do you have anything to say, Corryne?" Her voice was gentle, almost like it was when I attended her classes in my second year. I imagined another griffin was conducting her lessons while she was at the courthouse.

I hadn't thought about what I'd say. I didn't know I was allowed to speak during the meeting, as I was a minor, but I had never appeared before the council, so I had no basis for comparison.

I started to speak, and words tumbled out of me. I was unsure, and I could feel the walls close in on me as the council members stared.

"I—I'm Corryne," I stuttered. Then, realizing how I sounded, I took a deep breath and began again.

"I realize that I've caused a lot of trouble in our town, but I don't think I'm the cause of the dome's decline." I stared hard at Namon, but he was back to rolling his pencil across his desk.

I decided to address each of my mother's points. "I don't have to explain the origin of my species. I was raised to hate any being who wasn't a werewolf, and I did until the other supernaturals in my year showed kindness to me."

Davis held his hands tightly in front of him, and occasionally his eyes shifted to his wife, trying to silently communicate with her. She seemed to successfully ignore his stare, focusing on me as if she were waiting for an opportunity to jump in and help.

I took a deep breath. "Maureen of Tribe Werewolf seeks to officially disown me, and I agree with her."

Everyone in the room seemed to be affected by my statement. The council members snapped to attention, and Namon stopped rolling his pencil. I thought I saw my father try to steal a glance at me.

"Do you understand that you will be alone if we grant her request?" Aella asked. "Without a host family, you will be banished for your crimes, as there will be no adults to deliver punishment for your actions."

I faltered, and Lilith squeezed my hand. "I will accept responsibility for her."

Most of the council members turned to Davis. Aella continued to speak to Lilith and me.

"I commend your compassion, Lilith of Tribe Faerie," Aella spoke. "However, you are part of a union, and Davis must agree."

Lilith stared at her husband, but he wouldn't look at her. His face reddened, and Aella saved me from further humiliation by moving on.

"Let's see if Corryne will remain inside the dome before we place her in a new home," she offered.

The other council members seemed satisfied and allowed me to continue speaking. Once Aella waved me on, I tried to think about my mother's charges against me.

"I think Maureen of Tribe Werewolf" —I motioned to my parents— "was right to disown me. I just wish she had done it sooner." I was beginning to sound like a spoiled child, so I hurried through my reasoning. "As she stated, she knew I was different from other werewolves. She understood that my views weren't consistent with hers. However, she still kept me, attempting to mold prejudice into my mind. Had she given me to another werewolf family, I may not have rebelled so harshly."

That part of my argument seemed to carry some weight with Aella. She crossed her legs and sat back in her chair, ready to hear my next point.

"I don't really have a defense for my actions, except that I knew Rymon wasn't a suitable mate for me when I was young. I tried to fight against my feelings, but I couldn't bring myself to think of him as more than my friend."

It was a point I'd have to repeat. They needed to understand that I had no romantic feelings for Rymon.

"I don't know how many of you were expected to marry someone when you loved someone else." Davis set his jaw, and Lilith's nose climbed a little higher.

"Anyway, the wolf my parents wanted me to marry was my best friend. Even though I loved him as a friend, I couldn't feel something more for him. It wasn't fair to either one of us."

"But he loved you," Nava interjected. "Your mother said he adored you, so marrying him would have been fair."

I wondered if Nava had been in Rymon's position, and my feelings had challenged her ideas about the relationship between her mate and her. It was possible other beings wouldn't sympathize with me for the view I had expressed, as sticking strictly to the council's rules largely benefitted many beings.

"She didn't care about him," Namon mused, twirling his pencil in the air. "She deviated from our rules because she couldn't unite with a being who loved her."

I hated hearing that I was shallow. I had thought I should experience love and passion, but the council was completely against inter-uniting our species'.

"On the subject of Allistar the Unicorn," Aella began.

"He has expressed concern for the girl," Ledot said, surprising me.

Aella nodded. "Should we discuss his banishment, too?"

Namon scoffed. "Without the pup, I don't see a need for him to leave. He will marry within his species."

"You're only saying that because your son is one of her lovers," Sitali spoke up. It was clear that she didn't talk often, as every head turned to her. "Maybe we should bring him here, or did you send him to the caves?"

Namon glared at her. "My son's whereabouts are none of your concern, but since it has been broached, he is at school."

"And Corryne should be there, too," Lilith voiced. "Her only crime was falling in love."

"With two people?" Nava shook her head. "A being should love one person and unite with them."

I hurried to speak. "I agree. I want to love one being."

"Then which one do you love?" Nava challenged.

"I don't know," I answered, "but I want to have a chance to find out."

"Impossible," Namon spat. "This council will not grant you a free pass to destroy the institutions that kept our fortifications strong for decades."

"I think you're wrong," I argued. "I believe that something else is breaking down the dome."

"What is it then?" Ledot questioned. She was entertained by the proceedings, but it was the first time she had shown genuine interest.

"I think someone may have tampered with it on the day my class visited the talisman."

Namon was the only one who didn't react to my statement. He leaned back in his chair and crossed one leg over another. "And do you have proof to accompany these allegations?"

"No," I admitted. "But everything started to change on the day of our field trip."

Most everyone on the council started speaking at one time. I heard snatches of their conversation, but I couldn't follow one particular path.

"I told you something happened that day."

"Namon was right when he—"

"I don't think it was that at all."

"It reacted to her because she's a blood traitor!"

Through the melee, Ledot and Sitali sat calmly with their eyebrows raised. Ledot held up her hand and the chatter ceased. "We have discussed this issue at great length, but we have come to no solid conclusion. I believe we should focus on the matter at hand."

"But this is part of the matter," Nava stated. "If interloping weakens the dome, then this young one's actions could have sealed our doom. "Who was she with on the field trip? Had her heart been swayed on that day?"

Namon quickly distracted himself again. This time, he rolled a pen across his knuckles. He appeared uninterested, but we both knew who I had been around most on the day of the field trip, and Namon had put me with him.

On that day, though, I had only pitied Zaffron. My feelings had been bouncing giddily around Allistar.

Davis threw up his hands. "This is getting us nowhere! I've debated the dome's failure until I'm blue in the face, and I'm sick of it. Can we decide what we're going to do about the young one and be done with it?"

I had several other points I wanted to make, but the council members nodded along with Davis. If I spoke up about my rights and kept them in the courtroom longer, it might sway one of my supporters away from a positive vote for me.

Lilith and I were dismissed to our bench and my parents were instructed to wait in another area. During the next agonizing hour, I thought about many outcomes, and I feared almost all of them.

Banishment was one of the scariest sentences handed down by the council. Beings who were banished were led to the western end of the dome and released into the Forbidden Zone.

I had visited the area many times, but that particular part was a feeding ground for vampires. They could roam the entirety of the Forbidden Zone, but rarely did they have to feed past the part next to their neighborhood.

Some of the beings who had been banished may have made it to another area to hide, but most of them were devoured quickly. For the most part, the vampires kept their blood lust in check, but when a being was banished, the vampires staged a game for fun. With so many vampires on their trail, most beings were consumed in seconds. Very few had escaped.

I was so certain of my banishment that I had constructed a plan. I'd use my speed to try to outrun them, and I'd race to the lake. Vampires weren't fond of water, so I'd dive into the lake and take my chances with whatever had tried to drag me into its depths when Rymon had rescued me.

Finally, Ledot collected us again, and I tried not to think of her running after me with her unnatural speed after I was banished. I stood at the same podium, using it to support myself. My legs were shaking, and bile was steadily climbing my throat.

Aella looked sober, and I didn't find it reassuring. Most of the council wouldn't look at me, and I tried to avoid the vampires' eyes.

Aella banged the gavel on her desk. "We have officially reconvened on the matter of Corryne of Tribe Werewolf."

My father put his arm around my mother like they were waiting for the results of a contest. They didn't seem sad at all about losing a daughter.

Lilith held my hand. It was sweaty, and it had to be an uncomfortable experience for her, but she didn't let our connection slip.

Aella read from a paper in front of her. We used very little of the paper and writing utensils left to us when the dome was closed, but they had to record their decision.

"Corryne of Tribe Werewolf, this council has elected to grant the request of Kurt and Maureen of Tribe Werewolf. Your family ties are absolved, and you are no longer their daughter."

My mother erupted in celebration, a display was completely uncharacteristic of our species. She settled almost immediately, nodding at the council and thanking them for their "wise" decision.

The room started to spin, but a quick squeeze from Lilith's hand gave me enough support to level my gaze and resist the urge to faint. My breath caught in my throat, and I held back tears as I became an orphan.

Lilith gave an audible sigh. "I speak for Corryne."

My mother, or whatever she was now that we were estranged, turned for the first time and snapped at her. "They already told you that you couldn't have her without your husband's permission, and it doesn't look like he wants anything to do with her."

Davis opened his mouth, but Lycon placed a hand on his arm. "Kurt and Maureen of Tribe Werewolf no longer have a place at this hearing, as it has been declared that their responsibility for Corryne has ended."

It wasn't lost on me that Lycon left off a tribal designation. I was officially a ward of the dome, likely to be banished.

After the beings that had raised me were escorted out of the courtroom, the room was hushed. Each member of the council stared at me, and I felt the full weight of their decision. Lycon seemed especially pensive, as if the consequences were hurting him more than me.

Aella spoke. "As you know, Corryne, without parents to guide your punishment, there is only one option available to this council."

"I seek to dissolve my union," Lilith interrupted.

"What?" Davis said, startled.

Aella's hand went to her heart. "Lilith of Tribe Fayrie, your actions are noble—"

"And rash," Nava interjected.

Aella narrowed her eyes at Nava before she resumed talking, drawing out the first word to strengthen her authority to speak. "*But* it takes almost a year to dissolve a union, and we can't leave Corryne's situation in limbo that long. She will be an adult in another two weeks."

"It looks like the youngling will be a permanent resident of the Forbidden Zone," Namon said dismissively. "Though, I doubt the vampires will let her live long enough to enjoy the amenities there. He flicked his hand like he was sweeping the matter off his desk. "Boo-hoo, and all that."

"We take no pride in sealing the doom of supernaturals," Ledot spoke flatly.

"But you certainly don't argue when we release one into your hunting grounds," he countered, his eyebrow raised and a cruel smile tickling his lips.

"We are slaves to blood in much the same way as you are chained to your jewels," she replied evenly, fixing him in her steady gaze. "You should be careful with your speech, Namon the Impaler. You require rest, but I never have to close my eyes."

"Is that a threat?" he yelled at her, slamming his fist on the table.

Aella banged her gavel. "That's enough!" She rubbed her temples. "We've all been in this small room for too long today, and we need to dismiss."

The beings on the council nodded in agreement. After a few beats of silence, Aella addressed me.

"Corryne, you are hereby—"

"I'll take her."

It was a bold move. All eyes turned to the unexpected source of the voice.

Lycon smiled at me and winked. He looked pale and nervous about his decision, but he had saved me.

— · —

CHAPTER 31

I was as uncomfortable as Lycon looked as we walked out of the courthouse. He ambled down the steps, and I followed him, stopping at a bike rack.

"I ride my bicycle wherever I go," he told me, pointing to the ancient blue bike. "You can ride it if you want."

I shook my head.

"In that case," he said, "I'll walk home with you." He urged the bike out of the rack and pushed it alongside us as we wound down the streets to his house.

It was strange to hear Lycon call his home mine, too. I felt like I owed him my loyalty, but I wasn't sure how to pledge it to him.

"You saved my life," I said.

I must have looked at him with something close to hero worship because he shook his head rapidly. "You owe me nothing, Corryne." He glanced sideways at me and added, "Of Tribe Werewolf."

I realized that I still had a place and a title. Not only had he saved me from almost certain death, but he had given me the chance to be more independent. After I walked under the Glistening Tree, I wouldn't have to worry about uniting with another tribe member. He had no reason to try to unite me with another member of our species.

"I think your classes are almost over today, so do you wish to wait until tomorrow to resume them?"

I thought the drama in the courtroom was enough to last me a lifetime, and I was in no hurry to enter the rumors and sideways chatter at the school. I expressed my feelings to Lycon.

He let out a chuckle, but then he stared at me seriously. "I think that's wise."

After a few minutes of silence that I longed to fill with a comfortable conversation, Lycon said, "I've never had a child. I have a daughter now."

We had never embraced, but he tried an awkward hug. One of his hands was still steadying his bicycle, and I held tightly to Archard's journal. We laughed at our efforts of affection.

"I've always respected you," I told him.

He nodded. My words were a little more in line with the sentiments of our kind.

Davis had my suitcase and duffle bag delivered to Lycon's address, and as it was only a couple of streets away from the faerie's neighborhood, my personal items were waiting for me when we arrived. The sight of my luggage on Lycon's porch disheartened me.

Lilith had cried when she'd let go of my hand. She had been happy that Lycon had claimed me, but she was upset over my circumstances.

I wasn't concerned about Lilith, but she was going to have a serious conversation with Davis when they returned home. She had tried to end her decades-long union with him to save my life and give me a place in the dome. Even though it hadn't worked out, I promised myself I would always remember her sacrifice. And I'd never forget Davis's rejection.

After what I'd read in Archard's journal and the looks that passed between Davis and his wife, I knew Davis had loved a being from another race. At the very least, he'd become fixated with the mermaid Cascade. *Had she broken his heart?* I remembered from my classes that Davis was one of the beings present when the original documents for our government were signed. *Had he influenced the portion about marrying other creatures?*

Lycon had spoken, but I had been so wrapped up in my thoughts that I hadn't heard him. I used a passing car on the almost quiet street as an excuse.

"I said, 'Welcome home,'" he repeated. "One day, remind me to tell you what's under the gnome's red hat."

Lycon and I spent a couple of days in comfortable company before the vandalism started.

The dome depreciated a little each day, and the creatures who lived in it struggled to find a place to put their fear that had manifested into anger. I was certain Maureen, for I had called her that since she had estranged herself from me, and Davis were vocal on my part in the dome's deterioration.

If it was my fault, it was also the fault of every creature who hadn't married with their kind and produced offspring. Under their flawed rationale, Hamlet and Lycon had helped destroy the dome.

I'd seen the werewolf who was once my brother a couple of times on my way to school. He was driving home after his work shift. I'd stare at his car until he looked out his window, purposely avoiding me.

In classes, most of the other beings stared at me like they hadn't known me for the last decade. Fiona, Fallyn, and Bredek crowded around me in the halls and class, but lunches were still hard.

Rymon hadn't taken it well when my mother had told his family that I had been caught with Zaffron, and they all assumed I'd slept with him. The engagement was officially dissolved, and Rymon was encouraged to pursue another female in our tribe. Rudi was happy to break off her engagement to Mingan when Rymon showed her his attention. They sat in front of me at lunch, while Rymon told me he wished me no ill will. He held hands with Rudi throughout the meal, even though it made it almost impossible for them to enjoy their lunches. After they ate, I wasn't disgusted when they practically made out in front of us, but I was irritated that it was a show orchestrated to make me jealous.

Truthfully, I was happy for Rymon. I was a little upset with Rudi for the way she had treated Mingan, but I was glad she had decided to unite with Rymon. Mingan was one of the most intelligent beings in our year, and Rudi was purposely vague. It wasn't a good match, so Rudi had done Mingan a favor by ending their relationship.

Fiona and Fallyn doted on me and asked me to stay at their house. I visited during the day, but I was careful to leave before Davis returned from his council duties. Lilith always sent me away with a warm embrace and the best of the produce from their personal garden.

Lycon was a great cook, and he managed to use everything Lilith gave us. As we were meat-eaters, he dressed the colorful dishes with a good deal of protein. My favorite dish he prepared was a casserole. He told me that it was the first thing his mother had taught him to cook, but she had put tuna in it. If we wanted fish, we were limited to the trout and catfish in our waters, so he added chicken to the recipe.

After dinner, we had quiet time in front of the fireplace. I imagined it roaring during the winters before the dome had been erected. The seasons around us weren't terribly harsh, but there had been significant amounts of snow on the dome in the past. Now, it would fall through the opening onto the vampires' and unicorns' neighborhoods, but as it was late spring, I doubted we'd see snow until the protection the dome provided was completely diminished.

During our quiet times, I read more of Archard's journal. I felt like I understood him more. When I learned about him in class, he was like a distant historical figure covered by the dust of time. As I turned each page of his memoir, though, I felt a deeper connection to him. It was almost like we were friends who were getting to know each other. Sure, our connection was one-sided, but I was convinced I knew more about his inner feelings than anyone outside of Amalthea and Cyprus.

I could easily have given the book to Lycon and asked him to see the tome he kept under his chair, but I didn't. I let him keep his secret, especially after he shared the rest of them with me. The surprise he'd left under the gnome's hat to ward against vampires was truly remarkable!

One evening, after a hard day of school, I sat down on the blue loveseat with Archard's journal. I thought about Rymon and Allistar, but my mind settled on Zaffron. We'd passed each other in the halls, but he stared straight over my head. Anytime I was close to him, the students around us jeered. Their comments poked at my pride but not because I was hurt by their remarks. I was upset because Zaffron didn't defend my honor.

Of course, Namon was always nearby, dogging his son's footsteps, so I was given the privilege of a scowl or a sideways jab. Mostly, he said, "Dogs should be chained."

Since I had been deemed a problem, my movements were carefully watched. I couldn't sneak away and go to the room where Zaffron and I had often met.

I wondered what kind of punishment he'd had to endure. Namon was known for his cruelty, so I could only imagine that Zaffon was trying to fly under his radar at home. I shivered to think about the suffering Zaffon may have to go through.

Earlier that day, Zaffron and I had been at the recycler discarding the rest of our lunches. I expected him to ignore me, and it seemed he was going to leave. Then he dropped something I didn't see.

When he bent to pick it up, he said, "I'm glad the council didn't banish you. It would have been a challenge for me to rescue you." I remained in shocked silence as he stood, and it was easy to dismiss it all after he didn't meet my eyes.

Releasing my thoughts about Zaffron, I thumbed through the journal, and I arrived at one of the last entries. The script was a little harder to read, as if Archard had been upset when he wrote it.

"When I lie down at night, a thousand thoughts run through my mind. My heart twists in agony as I see the dome crushed under the army of King Kano. But how can I tell thousands of beings about a war that may or may not happen?

Some beings won't even be alive to see its destruction, but for most, they'd live in fear of their final days. They could even raise a panic that could turn the creatures on each other.

On the other hand, perhaps they could prepare to fight. But the numbers King Kano led were too many; the town's destruction was imminent.

Should I turn them all away and let them fortify their defenses in another way? When I thought of it, my mind's eye sent me a vision of supernaturals who were hunted and easily dispatched.

Should I imprison the elves in their wooded dominion? My visions tell me they can't be held without a jewel that has been lost in time for a millennium.

I torture myself until deep into the night, and my only reprieve is to write down these thoughts in a book. I plan to give it to Cyprus, and this journal to Amalthea, but I'll wait until I'm closer to the end.

Every day I wish my fate was avoidable, but I know the price of the spell. It will take everything I have to make sure the beings inside the dome are protected. In doing so, I will protect my sister, and our mother predicted her destiny was greater than mine.

When I'm finally able to sleep, my mother visits my dreams. She speaks of the mate I have yet to meet and calms my fears of the future. To date, I haven't met a being as splendid as the one she described, but I know my feelings will show as soon as we meet.

I keep searching for a way out, but my need to serve others prevents me from having selfish desires. My altruism will be fatal, and I hope my sister will live through it with happy memories of me. I hope she remembers the lakeside chats in the lily boat and the dragon fruit cakes instead of my impatience with her. It was truly my tortured mind that inspired my rants and not my lack of love for her. She will always be my first concern, even over the one my mother promised was meant to be mine.

I stopped reading and reflected. Archard was the most powerful wizard of his age, yet he doubted himself and his abilities. He planned to give Cyprus his journal of premonitions, but the journal I held had never reached Amalthea. The only difference was that Cyprus had lived while Amalthea had most likely perished during the closure of the dome.

Could the book under Lycon's chair uncover the secrets of Archard's visions? Did it tell the time and location of the breach? Could the failing dome be King Kano's influence after all?

Just as I was going to risk asking my adopted father to peer at Cyprus' book again, a loud crash sounded. The breaking glass shattered around us, causing me to scream in surprise.

We were under attack.

—·—

CHAPTER 32

My hands went instinctively to my face, and Lycon pulled me to the floor. He covered me with his body, but no other destruction followed.

After a few moments, we rose, shaking from the rush of adrenaline. Lycon instructed me to call the griffins while he inspected the house. Bricks had rolled just beyond the broken windows. Three windows had been broken at the front of the house as if the criminals had hastily thrown the bricks and fled.

The griffins responded to the call, and I was glad my brother wasn't with them. Azarra recognized me, and she gently asked questions about my experience.

I understood the reason Hamlet was so infatuated with her. Her beauty went beyond her unique plumage and settled in her compassion for others. I wished he had united with her, and to my horror, I started asking her some uncomfortable questions.

"I'm surprised you aren't united," I said. "Have you ever had a husband?"

She had just finished asking me what I'd been doing before the vandalism occurred. I'd answered, and the additional inquiry had rolled out of my mouth.

Azarra's mouth dropped open a little, but she recovered quickly. "I was married, but he passed beyond my reach several years ago."

I instantly colored. I'd thought she'd been single while my brother obsessed over her, but she had already been taken. With her shining beauty and good nature, it wasn't a surprise.

I loved the way griffins described the death of their loved ones. It was like the other person had slipped into an area just beyond their scope, but one leap could rejoin them.

"I'm so sorry."

She patted my hand. "The wound will never heal, but it no longer bleeds freely." She brightened. "And we had a daughter. She is close to your age, and her flight patterns are so much like her father's that my heart swells with happiness."

I could see Azarra's pride in her offspring, and I wondered if Hamlet had been jealous of her little family. If they'd had a daughter around my age, did being around me remind him that there was more than one obstacle when it came to his infatuation with Azarra?

"Are you certain you are well?" Azarra asked. "Your face is the shade of a tomato."

I decided to be honest. "I'm embarrassed that I've asked you a personal question. I'm sorry."

She smiled. "You would be shocked at the things I hear. Stress will make you do many uncharacteristic things."

After the griffins left, I helped Lycon clean up. No matter how careful we were, shards of glass poked us, but we healed quickly. It prompted me to start a conversation I'd tried to have with him.

"Did you ever train for battle?"

Lycon paused with his back hunched over a pile of glass. He resumed sweeping it into a dustpan with a broom as he replied.

"No, Corryne, I'm not battle-ready. I was raised by a peaceful being, and I'd like to think I model her behavior." He waited for a beat and spoke again.

"Do you see this room?" He motioned to the floor, where sharp fragments glinted. "This is nothing compared to the destruction of war. War will leave some of the ones you love dead and the rest of them in constant danger. Is that what you want?"

I thought I had an answer ready. "No. I want us to stand and fight. I don't want to run for the rest of my life. War is scary, and I'm not battle-ready either, but everyone will be in constant danger anyway. Shouldn't we make a stand?"

"Didn't you read the book I gave you?" he shouted, surprising me. "Didn't you see the capabilities of mermaids and elves? Sure, the druids are a little hardier than humans, but mermaids can focus attacks with their songs, and elves are almost impossible to kill."

"We have vampires," I countered.

"How many, though? Are the hundreds of vampires under the dome enough to overcome the thousands of elves ready to attack?"

It was clear I wasn't going to win him over to my rationale, so I stayed quiet. I didn't expect him to speak to me for the rest of the night, so I jumped when he changed the subject. His back was turned to me, so he didn't witness my surprise.

"I'll have to find a way to strengthen the defenses on the property," he said. "Until then, I'll walk you to class every day."

It seemed reasonable. There was unrest in our neighborhood, as many werewolves believed that I should have been banished on the morning my mother caught Allistar in my bed, but after I was found with Zaffron, almost everyone felt that I should be gone. The bricks were just the first physical attacks. I had already suffered through many verbal ones, and Lycon had probably endured ill remarks, too.

Lycon and I went to the same building every day, so it didn't bother me. I'd shift my schedule a little to accommodate him walking with me instead of biking there before I left.

Lycon ripped some old boxes and fixed them over the windows. "That should hold them until I can have them fixed."

I envied his faith in the flimsy material. I knew that if someone wanted to come in, there would be very little on Lycon's property that could keep them out.

—·—

CHAPTER 33

The day before Glistening Day was a free day for our year. If we came to class, there were games and other fun activities, but we could also stay home. No one counted the absence against us, and it could be used as a time for deep reflection.

Almost every being attended class for fun, and I'd had every intention of being part of it until I'd almost been banished. I didn't want to see the haughty stares and hear the jabs about my near banishment all day. Fallyn, Fiona, and Bredek would have felt the need to shelter me—or worse—defend me all day, and it wouldn't have been fair to them. I wanted my friends to have fun.

Lycon didn't question my decision to stay home or urge me to go. He let me rest while he ate his breakfast and packed his lunch. He must have sensed that I was awake, but he didn't disturb me before he left. The repetitive squeak of his bicycle pedals, as he moved down the sidewalk, lifted a weight from my shoulders.

I didn't feel comfortable roaming around his house all day, and I was a little disappointed when I felt under the chair for Cyprus' book. I realized that my new guardian cared about me, but he didn't fully trust me, as he had taken the book with him or hidden it somewhere else.

I took a walk around the neighborhoods, leaving my own quickly. The faerie's houses were lively, with small offspring who had yet to grow their wings jumping off diving boards into pools of bubbles and foam. Happy parents cheered as their progeny landed their first dives with their arms extended into the wind.

"Look at her form!"

"Watch how he lifts off his feet! He's more skilled than me!"

I enjoyed hearing the positive comments, and it made me long for a time when I'd received gentle nods of approval from my own parents. I didn't crave the affection, but I wished they had been less exuberant about excommunicating me.

I didn't know I was walking in the unicorn neighborhood until a familiar shadow joined mine. I was used to the crimson hues that fell around us, but I was angered by the person who cast the shadow. I moved away from him, eager to put distance between us.

"I was glad you weren't banished," he said.

I'd heard the same comment from Zaffron, but his tone had been less forced.

"Yeah, same to you, Allistar," I responded gruffly. "Too bad you didn't have to stand trial for your own infractions."

"My parents punished me."

I glared at him. "And it looks like they're around to enforce it."

"You don't have to bite my head off," he said. "You were betrothed, and you were caught with another being."

"Yeah, and the council knows you were with Mariam, but you weren't kicked out of your home, and she's a *human*!"

He shook his head condescendingly. "It seems you have some anger issues."

I resisted the urge to show him my new claws. I had started to shift, and even though my incisors hadn't developed, my temper was unpredictable.

A smile inched up his face, and he had the nerve to chuckle at my oversensitivity. "You know, I still care for you." He reached out to play with my hair. "We could hang out at my house and—"

"Not a chance," I replied, batting his hand away. "I'd rather kiss a frog."

"I guess a lizard *is* pretty close," he mused. "How is Zaffron these days?"

"Better than you!" I yelled. "He's always been better than you!"

He tsked. "See. Anger issues."

I threw up my hands and stormed down the road. He shifted and caught up with me easily.

"Why do you like Zaffron better than me?" he asked. There was a hint of vulnerability in his voice that surprised me.

"Why do you like Mariam better than me?"

"I don't."

I snorted. "You could've fooled me. Why were you with her that night?"

"Which—" he started but when he saw me snarl, he backpedaled. "I was with her because I thought you didn't want me."

"What are you talking about?"

"Well, you were betrothed to Rymon and never talked to me about it. I thought it was over between us."

I stopped, staring at the ground. Allistar was right. I'd never called him and explained the situation; I'd just assumed he knew that I still wanted to be with him.

"I haven't seen Mariam since the night you were arrested."

"I wasn't arrested," I said irritably. "I was escorted back to my... I was driven away."

Allistar touched my arm and caressed my shoulder. "I was so worried about you."

I tried to shrug him off me, but he resisted. "You ran away!"

"Only because I thought you were right behind me!" He dragged his hand down to my elbow and pulled me to him. I let his arms encircle my waist. There was no strength there, but I felt like he cared. "I never would have left you behind." We kissed, and he lifted me off my feet.

He walked me to his house, and I let him kiss me through the morning and most of the afternoon. We talked about our future and made plans for it. But the whole time he talked about having one male and one female offspring and working at the healthcare facility with his parents, I was only half-interested. I was still enamored with Allistar's violet eyes and silver hair, but something pulled at my mind, nudging me to recognize it. I pushed it away, but it kept coming back. I knew what I was avoiding but refused to think about it. To give it thought would give it credence, and I needed to stay in the world where the decisions that had driven my parents away wouldn't have been in vain.

"I'll be a good mate," Allistar promised as we spoke over the phone. It was late in the evening, and the sun had already dipped behind the mountains.

I pressed my swollen lips together. They still tasted like his lavender kisses. "Okay."

"Are you going to do it?"

It took me a minute to realize what he meant. "I'll ask the Glistening Tree to turn me into the form I most desire."

"Good," he said, seeming to relax a little. "When it happens, I'll use my wish."

"What?"

Allistar had been expecting my confusion. "The council may try to send us to the Forbidden Zone, so I'll wipe their minds. I'll make them think you were always a unicorn."

It was one of the most selfless things Allistar had ever said to me. "But what about Lycon? He adopted me. And Rymon was my best friend; he never would have been friends with a unicorn."

At first, the line was silent. Then he whispered, "He was my friend."

I didn't pick up on Allistar's wounded feelings. "But he was my *best* friend."

"And now he hates you."

I was knocked off balance by the venom in his tone, so I traced our conversation in my mind. I finally arrived at the point I thought I'd hurt him.

"I'll be happy to be a unicorn. Thank you for using your first wish on me."

He was silent again, but when he spoke, it was much more positive. "Most unicorns give their first wish to their spouse. You'll have a first wish, too, and I have a few suggestions about how you can use it."

"I bet you do."

After I ended the call, I joined Lycon in the kitchen for my Glistening meal. I'd have breakfast the next morning, but most younglings were too nervous to eat right before they walked around the tree, so their parents made a grand meal the night before the big event.

The venison steak had been grilled to perfection, and even though I wasn't a fan of asparagus, I tolerated it for the sake of my guardian. When I finished my food, he brought out a large cheesecake and cut a piece that almost looked like it was half the cake.

"I know how young ladies like their sweets."

I laughed good-naturedly. "We do, but I don't know if my stomach can hold all this."

Later that evening, as we sat by the fireplace, Lycon closed his book and stared at me. I shut my book and gave him my full attention, hoping he'd show me Cyprus's book.

"I want to pass on some advice," he said. "It's not handed down through my family, but I can see some things in you that I once saw in myself."

I'd never really compared myself to Lycon. He was a werewolf, but beyond that, we seemed different.

"I know you don't understand why I would rather run and hide than fight, but there was a time when I fought everyone and everything."

I couldn't imagine my peaceful guardian standing up to anyone. I pictured him in front of his teachers and classmates with his teeth barred and claws extended, but the image fizzled away.

"I was still young when Kano rose to power. I was in love, and I foolishly believed that I could rip apart the army of elves and druids easily."

He locked eyes with me. "I knew our best chance was to stand and fight, but I couldn't rally enough beings who believed the same." He took a deep breath. "When Kano's army ran into the town, I was the first one on the front line." He strummed the pages of his closed book nervously.

"The druids were easy to kill. I just slashed their throats or tore off their heads. But the elves... I killed one." He made a motion of grabbing the air with both his hands. I imagined that he saw the elf in front of him in his mind. "I popped its head off and threw it to the ground, but it came right back up and drew its weapon."

In the book Lycon had given me, there were many details about elves and their near immortality. They drew their energy from the earth, and the woods and soil replenished them. There were only a couple of ways to kill them, and without a certain jewel that hadn't been seen for a millennium, it was almost impossible to best them in battle.

He lifted his shirt, revealing a scar over his belly. Through the mass of dark hair surrounding it, a prominent white imperfection shined in the room's low light.

"She thought she'd killed me." He put his shirt back in place and stared at his lap.

"Before that point in my life, I always felt as invincible as the elf proved she was, but that injury showed me something." He lifted his eyes. "It showed me my own mortality."

His eyes sparkled with tears he was too proud to shed. "I lay on the ground and watched the beings fall around me. A faerie lay at my side, with his green eyes open and his brains spilling onto the ground, and a troll almost dropped her club on my head when she fell, her arm cut off at the shoulder." He rubbed his temples. "I watched dragons and unicorns as they were shot out of the sky, and my own brethren were torn apart by silver-tipped arrows."

He cleared his throat, looking back up at me with his fingers resting on the sides of his head. "I was there when your grandmother was slain."

My heartbeat sped up and marched in my ears. "You knew my grandmother?"

He stared at me miserably. "I was the one who encouraged her to fight, but I never would have talked her into it if I had known it would leave your mother an orphan."

His lips trembled, and I thought more emotion would follow, but he picked up his book again, seeming to draw strength from the fictional story by an unknown author. "I am so sorry."

"Does my mother know?"

He shook his head. "She'd never understand. I had every intention of telling her, but she grew with such prejudices." He laughed. "I was surprised when she married your father. He was a peaceful man, much like me, but she had a way of shifting his ideals."

I nodded my head in agreement. Even though I was still angry with my father, I agreed with Lycon's assessment of him. I thought I knew the reason he allowed my mother's opinions to infiltrate his own beliefs, though. He loved her, and she had the stronger personality out of the pair. Most of the time he agreed with her to keep the peace, but after he acquiesced for so long, his support was assumed.

"Your grandmother, Louve, was fierce in battle," he continued. "She ripped through twelve druids before she was injured and went on fighting until the elf who was ready to deliver my death blow noticed her.

"I watched them fight, and Louve grabbed a chunk of her shoulder with her teeth and spat it on the ground. The elf drew an arrow and stuck it into her thigh, smiling as she watched your grandmother lose vitality. She slung her on top of me as if she were making a pile."

"You watched her die," I said solemnly.

"Not before she begged me to get a message to the werewolf caring for her daughter. She wished for her daughter, Maureen, to remain in her care."

He bent forward, putting his elbows on his knees. "I don't know if it was the weight of her message or my will to live that carried me through. All I know was that I passed out from the pain, and when I woke, I was healing in a care facility. I begged to see Cyprus, and he told me the werewolf who had been caring for Maureen had died, but her husband, Sampson, had assumed her guardianship. I was glad until I learned about the depth of his hatred."

He looked up at me. "I'm not saying your life would have been much different, but maybe if I had raised your mother—"

"You can't think that way. Most werewolves share the same prejudices, and she would have reacted the same way—even if you would have raised her. I think it's something that's in certain beings, like it's passed in the genetic code or something."

He shook his head. "I don't believe prejudice is innate. I think it is learned." He put the book on the table beside him. "But that brings me to my advice."

I waited for him to speak. He opened and closed his mouth twice, finally resolving the words he wanted to say.

"Every being is precious. If you overlook any of them, you will miss beautiful opportunities.

"I had a love more precious than the moon, but I let our differences keep me from uniting us. I wish I could go back and correct my mistake, but time and distance have separated us."

"I'm sorry," was the only response I thought was appropriate.

"Don't apologize on my behalf," he said. "I made my decisions, and I suffer the consequences for them every day I wander this old house alone."

I put my hand on his arm. "You're not completely alone."

He smiled sadly, covering my hand with his. "I know, Corryne, and if you aren't embarrassed by this sentimental old being, I'd like to be present for your Glistening tomorrow."

"I can't think of anyone I'd want there more than you," I told him.

I had been warned that the time before my Glistening would be confusing, but I hadn't been fully prepared for war, subterfuge, fickle boyfriends, or my roaming teenage emotions.

I spent the night before my Glistening lying awake in bed, thinking about King Kano's threat, Namon's betrayal, and my feelings for the being who held my heart. Finally, I settled on a course of action that I hoped would benefit all the beings under Archard's dome.

—·—

Chapter 34

I stared at the Glistening Tree. It stood in magnificent splendor, the deep gold shimmering like running flakes of sand.

Most of the council members stood at the opposite end of the tree, patiently waiting for the newest citizen of the species. Aella and Nava smiled and congratulated each graduate, Ledot and Davis smiled tightly as each being passed, and Namon appeared bored.

I watched as my classmates were sprinkled with a lustrous glitter and emerged in their true form. There were no surprises. Every being became the same kind as their parents before them. It seemed I was the only one with a decision.

Allistar and Rymon had held back, and they were watching me. I gave nothing away as I inched closer in line to the tree where I would decide the course of my life. My parents were absent from the sea of proud faces, but I knew Lycon was there.

Allistar took his turn and emerged in iridescent light. Rymon and Zaffron casually strolled around the tree and manifested into their forms. It was as natural for them as uncurling a fisted hand.

A handful of trolls and faeries remained in the line with me. My reluctance started to look like trepidation, so I moved behind Bredek and waited for him to complete his transformation.

All eyes were on me as my feet took the steps toward my destiny. I heard whispers and convinced myself that the onlookers had guessed my thoughts. The crowd stood still, though, silently watching another being accept their chosen form.

The Glistening Tree's leaves rustled. It was now or never.

I sent my feelings out in waves, like the ripples in standing water after a stone had been dropped into its stillness. The branches lifted lightly as if to say, *Are you sure?* I closed my eyes and nodded, waiting for the dusty particles around me to shift my form and my future.

The shift was painful. The bones in my body cracked and refitted to my joints at different angles. I cried out, but my ears heard a powerful roar instead of a desperate plea for the agony to end. What took only moments felt like it lasted for days. My torture was intense, but—finally—my legs moved as if they were powered by someone else. Each step shook the ground, and the air around me was thick, like the steam billowing up after lifting the cover off a boiling pot.

An uncomfortable sensation rose into my chest, like I had eaten too much of the candy meat stew my mother had loved to make. I opened my mouth to belch and relieve some pressure in my throat, but fire as hot as a furnace rocketed from my mouth. It singed the trees around the gaping spectators.

Davis was the first to leave; his disappointment showed clearly on his face. Allistar and Rymon had shifted into their human forms and looked at me with their mouths slightly open. Zaffron stood beside them, wearing no recognizable expression.

I willed myself into shifting back, and it was as easy as pulling my hoodie over my head. I stood in place, thinking about where I belonged. I should have been going to the pack of werewolves, but they all looked at me with disdain. There were only three dragons lined up in their designated area, but they didn't invite me to join them.

I found Lycon's face, and his smile encouraged me. He put a thumb in the air, an old gesture from the human world that meant *Good job!*

I was ready to accept my fate and took a breath to steel my nerves. Before I could inch a step in either direction, Namon barreled down on me, grabbed my arm, and whisked me away.

— · —

CHAPTER 35

Now, facing the leaders of each tribe, I had challenged him. I had agreed to fight Namon the Impaler, whose claws were so deadly that he was rumored to have skewered humans on them in battles older than several generations of werewolves. He didn't shift, though. He only held me with his coal-black eyes as he descended, ready to defend his title.

I shifted gracefully, straightening my spine and lifting my head with pride. I unfurled my wings and unleashed my first battle cry as a dragon. Flames danced across my skin as my body morphed into my chosen form.

Namon flipped a sword in his hand. The steel glinted in the light, but there was something on the surface of the blade that caused me to wince. Silver wasn't a good metal for swords, but was the steel lined with the metal that had destroyed my ancestors? Alone, the sword would kill a dragon, but the silver would defeat a werewolf. He couldn't have anticipated my turn, so why did Namon possess such a sword? *Had he killed werewolves, too?*

My resolve strengthened. I returned to my previous shape and matched his stance. A vampire guard gave me her sword; I wasn't the only one who didn't like Namon. The hilt was heavy and decorated with a crest and filigree. I struggled to hold the steel, but if I stayed in a human form, it was the only defense left to me.

His body crouched into an easy fighting stance, his arms and legs poised for attack. He wasn't shifting; he didn't have to turn into a dragon to defeat me.

Before I could strike the first blow, Rymon stepped in front of me. "I evoke the right of substitution," he called out.

"No!" I shouted. "This is *my* fight!"

Rymon glanced back at me, and the love he felt for me was reflected in his eyes. I'd thought our friendship had ended, but he'd only been hurt. "Not anymore."

He lunged at Namon, shifting in the air. Rymon hadn't been close enough to be repelled by the silver lining on the steel, and when the blade went through him, Rymon reverted into a human form.

"No!" I screamed. I ran to my friend, laying his head in my lap and gasping for air between sobs. "Please! No!"

Rymon stared at me as his body convulsed. Namon pulled the sword from his stomach. "Move away," he directed me calmly. "I need to end his suffering."

"You should suffer!" I screamed at him. "You are a blood traitor and a liar!"

Namon stared down at me with a somber expression. "He doesn't deserve this pain after demonstrating such bravery. Dragons don't allow other creatures to suffer."

Rymon looked up at me. He tried to speak as blood bubbled out of his mouth. He started choking on it, but his eyes begged me to understand what he wanted to tell me.

Ledot and Sitali left through the grand doors. They almost flew out of them; the temptation to feed almost overwhelmed them. Zaffron slipped into the room as they left. He took in the scene as he stood beside the door.

"No!" I screamed at no one in particular. I covered my friend and shielded him from whatever mercy Namon was ready to give him. It would have been more compassionate to have thrown down his sword before fighting a new werewolf with no battle experience.

A hand touched my shoulder. "Let me."

I shrugged away from the touch before I registered the owner of the voice. When I looked up, my tear-streaked face met Allistar's moist eyes. The starbursts were swirling with the new magic.

"It's my fault we're here," he told me. "Please let me make it right."

It all hit me in a flash. Allistar wanted to be with Mariam. He would have done anything to bring down the barrier.

"I touched the necklace," he admitted. "I asked it to destroy the dome." Two tears rolled down his cheeks. "I didn't think this would happen." He motioned to Rymon.

"King Kano knows we're vulnerable," Lycon spoke. "Did you think of the repercussions?"

Allistar shook his head, openly weeping. "I only thought of Mariam."

My heart should have dropped at his admission, but if I was honest, I knew it all along. *Why had he taken me to a house where a unicorn and a human lived?* We weren't there to learn about a way for us to be together; Allistar was finding a way to be with Mariam.

Allistar stood and spread his arms. His body emitted golden rays as his form shifted. I was on his right, and my hand reached out to run down his silky flank. Instead of touching his horn to Rymon, though, Allistar lifted it into the air. We couldn't hear most of his words with our ears because he was no longer in a human form, but they reverberated through the room and some of them echoed into our minds. "I wish I had not touched the necklace."

Lycon rose from his seat with his hand up as if he hoped to stop Allistar or issue a warning, but the effects of Allistar's wish were instantaneous. Lycon's mouth closed, and a serene expression crossed over his face. He lowered his body back into his chair with no memory of his objection.

The air in the room rang, and everything came into a surreal focus. Then I blinked and took in the changes. Ledot and Sitali sat in their positions; no blood had been spilled, so they weren't concerned. Allistar and Rymon flanked me, and Rymon was unhurt. He smiled at me as if edging me to proceed. I kept myself from crying again, but traces of my tears still lingered on my face.

Allistar's wish affected other aspects of my life. Dual memories flooded my mind as I accepted two timelines. Thoughts pelted my mind like bullets. I remembered my make-out sessions with Allistar, but we had never been more than friends in the current timeline. Rymon had been angry with me both times I had chosen someone instead of him, but after Zaffron and I announced our relationship, he remained my friend and encouraged me to become a dragon. My parents had still disowned me, and Lycon had claimed me as his own. My choice was the same; I could feel the fire burning inside my chest.

Zaffron stood before me, speaking to the elders. "We beseech you, in the name of the Glistening Tree and the power it holds, please allow Corryne to move seamlessly into Tribe Dragon."

Namon crossed his arms. "This is utterly ridiculous! This is not how a dragon is born!"

"But father," Zaffron protested. "The number of dragons continues to fall. We need to reproduce, but we are limited by—"

"I understand our genetics!" his father spat at him. "But who would marry this"—he sneered— "*mixed breed?*"

"Me," Zaffron spoke without pause. "We can take our vows immediately."

I lost my breath and started to choke on my saliva. Rymon slapped his hand on my back, and Allistar steadied me.

Thoughts rushed into my mind that detailed stolen moments with Zaffron. Most of my memories with him in the old timeline remained untouched and mingled with new experiences of long talks into the night and the feeling of his arms wrapped around me.

The dome wasn't on the verge of disappearing, but the defenses it provided were slowly weakening. Allistar's touch hadn't been the only thing that had started the collapse of our protection. Perhaps Macon and Lily had been right. Maybe other beings had intermingled, causing a decline in the magic that powered the talisman. Allistar's actions in the other timeline may have sped up an already diminishing power.

New memories came to me that mingled with my experiences with the talisman. I had been having strange dreams about the necklace, and it had been trying to communicate with me through them. I had visited the cave that housed the talisman the night before my Glistening, but my mind hadn't completely caught up with this timeline, so I was unaware of what had happened.

There was still a breach in the south end of the dome's barrier, and Zaffron and I had witnessed his father make trades with the same two druids. Because of Allistar's wish, though, Zaffron and I shared our first kiss after one of those exchanges. I absent-mindedly touched my lips. I had never been involved with Allistar.

"It's what is in your heart," Allistar whispered knowingly. "Believe me; I checked it." He nodded at Zaffron and added, "He doesn't remember it any other way."

"Who else knows?"

"Just us," he replied and glanced up at the tribe elders. "And maybe a few of them. Especially the ones that have experience with old magic."

Namon stormed out of the room, his black robes billowing behind him. The rest of the council stared down at Zaffron until Lycon looked at them briefly and spoke. "In the absence of Namon the Impaler, the council grants Zaffron the Silver-Tongued and Corryne the Resilient permission to take your vows at your leisure."

I smiled. Now that I was a dragon, I had been given my formal name. As the leader of my former tribe and my last guardian, it seemed fitting that Lycon had given it to me.

Zaffron took my hand and led me into the Grand Galley triumphantly. The two timelines converged, and I wondered if anyone knew the other one existed besides Allistar and me. *And why hadn't Allistar wiped my mind with the wish? Why had he wanted me to remember the other timeline?*

Allistar, Rymon, Zaffron, and I met Fiona, Fallyn, Pat, Puck, and Bredek at a large marble pillar as if it had been part of a plan. The sounds of the celebration covered our deception.

I gave Allistar a sideways glance. *Were Zaffron's feelings for me real, or was he only playing a part?* If the lingering magic still allowed him to read my thoughts, Allistar committed to nothing, looking away from my eyes.

I chastised myself for my pitying concerns about lost love and settled into the plan. We were all too new and weak in our developing powers. We had to find a way to beat Namon without challenging him openly.

"Did they believe you?" Fiona asked Zaffron.

"Yes," Zaffron said, holding my hand up as if to prove a point. "Now it's time to take my father down from the inside."

Mummers traveled through the parents and newly Glistened beings at the entrance. They parted like waves, allowing a figure to move between them.

Purple robes dragged the floor, the heavy velvet an uncommon fabric for my time, but it laid beautifully on his olive skin. His dark hair was meticulously clipped, and rugged stubble brushed his chin and jaw. Thin lips rested beneath a straight nose, and broad shoulders carried his cloak as he stood with perfect posture. His cerulean eyes searched me, and I knew him, even though we'd never met.

He took my hand and kissed it, sending shivers of electricity through every nerve of my body. My heart tore instantly, one side still belonging to Zaffron, but the other side was drawn to the intriguing being before me.

"Archard," I spoke with a stronger voice than I felt.

I thought he had died when he had cast the spell over the town. The only reason I could find for his sudden appearance was that he had preserved himself in the talisman. But if Allistar hadn't touched the necklace, who was responsible for the dome's declining protection? Who woke up the magician responsible for its creation? And why was Archard looking at me like he had always known and loved me?

He held my gaze another moment before he turned to the other beings in my group, a commanding clip in his tone. They were as baffled by his presence as me but seemed to know him from the stories we learned in classes.

"The dome is failing," he said. "It's almost time for the battle to begin."

To be continued...

— • —

DID YOU ENJOY THIS BOOK?

Did you like Under Archard's Dome? If so, please leave a review on Amazon, Goodreads, and BookBub! Just a few words, like *I enjoyed it!* can really help an author (and bring a ray of sunshine into my day).

This book is the first in a series, so look for the next book in the Under Archard's Spell Series, releasing in 2024!

— · —

Closing Remarks

No matter what has happened in my past, I love everyone. We are all struggling to live in the world we exist in today. If we're doing well now, it may not have always been that way.

My story may be a fantasy, but it applies to certain social issues. Replace the beings as humans with different skin colors, religious values, or beliefs, and you have a situation similar to the tragedies that have been played throughout human history.

No one ever had peace and happiness with hate in their hearts. Love and forgiveness may not solve every problem, but I'm willing to give it a try. I hope you join me.

— • —

About the Author

Courtnee Turner Hoyle is the author of the award-winning My Brother's Keeper and Solomon's Tears. She also penned the Pale Woods Mystery Series, It's About Time Series, and Rasputin's Dynasty Trilogy. Courtnee lives in Northeast Tennessee with her children. She graduated with two undergraduate degrees and a Master of Arts in Teaching from East Tennessee State University. Courtnee enjoys reading, writing, and any reasonable music. She spends her days in comfortable chaos, avoiding sweet tea, chocolate, and unannounced visitors. Follow her on Instagram @pale_woods_mysteriesand visit her website: www.courtneeturn erhoyle.com

— · —

ACKNOWLEDGEMENTS

My daughter, Tosha, has always been my biggest fan. I'm so lucky to have her support. She has designed my website, and she promotes my work, but most of all, she gets as excited about my characters as me.

Avalee, I hope you continue to write stories. Your belief in me has been one of the driving factors in my creativity.

Stereling and Kinidy, I wrote a fantasy novel for you to read. I hope you can identify with some of the characters!

Journee, thank you for asking me about my books each day. It pushes me to make more progress.

Legende, a small amount of your spirit is reflected in the pages. I released the book on your birthday because you and I love were-wolves. Thanks to you and Journee, my life is interesting.

Jubilee and Rynegade are my calm heroes. Thank you for the balance.

I write so that my children will be proud of me, and to leave a legacy of stories for them. Speaking of Legacee, thank you for getting excited over the covers of my books, even if you never plan to read them.

Thank you, Mama, for your dedicated beta reading. Your input and support are invaluable!

Taylor Dawn, Sweet15 Designs, LLC designed the cover for the book. Thank you for the time you took to select the perfect background and for not including your "horrifying griffin" in the final proof.

I appreciate all my advanced readers in Book Bindings. Each of you is amazing, and I am grateful for your thought-provoking reviews. Linda, Judy, Elaine, Lisa, and Tammy have shared some valuable thoughts with me.

Stephanie Edwards has been an amazingly supportive friend during the last year. I've enjoyed our conversations and YouTube videos. I'm honored that she asked me to help her interview other authors on our Bless Your Books Blog.

And to you, dear reader, thank you for continuing this journey with me. Without you, my stories would stay in my close family, but you have the power to give them more life!

—·—

More of Courtnee's Titles

Hollis's Hobby

Can you trust your lover?

After an abusive childhood and soul-splitting heartbreak, Hollis hovers around her hometown, secretly killing the men who are unfortunate enough to fall for her charms, until her lonely friend, Josie, asks Hollis to move in with her. Hollis attempts to drop "Holli", the alter ego who dispatches her unsuspecting lovers, but she finds it difficult to function as a teacher when she sees the evidence of abuse on the people she values. In an effort to veer away from her murderous path, Hollis forms a relationship with the father of one of her students, Quillen, but he's running from a secret Hollis may not understand.

Hollis's sad and twisted past has never been unearthed, but will Quillen's influence cause her to dig up details that could risk her capture? When all Hollis's secrets threaten to come to the surface, will she continue to live under the guise she's created, or will Hollis's hobby be revealed?

— · —

More of Courtnee's Titles

PALE WOODS PARANORMAL SUSPENSE SERIES

SOLOMON'S TEARS
Courtnee Turner Hoyle

Are the ghosts in her house or in her mind?
Ketron Gouge is puzzled when she feels like one of her children is missing. A quick check calms her panicked mind, but the uncomfortable thought continues to concern her.

Ketron and her husband, Marvin, bought a home they hoped would be perfect for their growing family. Soon, however, Marvin develops a drinking problem and Ketron becomes more anxious about the mysterious shadows and crying in the house. Most of her five children seem to be conscious of the uncanny events, giving credence to Ketron's worries, but her best friend and therapist think it may be a product of her overstressed mind.

Ghosts from her past and memories of her childhood tumble to the surface, reminding her of her mentally unstable mother, and she begins to wonder if there's truth to the nagging idea that someone is missing. And when she begins hearing and seeing things in her house, she thinks it may be time to accept an inescapable truth.

www.ingramcontent.com/pod-product-compliance
Lightning Source LLC
Chambersburg PA
CBHW031335170626
46807CB00002B/702